Rondo

Tell Cotten

Also by Tell Cotten

Confessions of a Gunfighter
Entwined Paths
Cooper

Dedication
To my parents, Leonard and Jan

Cover Art:
Marcy Meinke/Converse Printing & Design
www.ConversePrinting.com
mike@converseprinting.com

Solstice Publishing - www.solsticepublishing.com

Prologue

Jeremiah Batch was an old black man. Two years back, he inherited a small ranch when his boss, Steve Hardin, was killed.

The ranch wasn't much, but it was all he had. So, when his cows came up missing, he didn't take it lightly. He loaded his Colt, saddled his horse, and rode out to Ike Nash's ranch headquarters.

He pulled up in front of the house, and several ranch hands gathered around him. Ike Nash wasn't there, but his son Tanner was.

Tanner was tall and slim and arrogant.

Jeremiah noticed that he held a Henry rifle, and the hammer was pulled back.

"Tanner," he said. "I need to look through your Pa's herd."

"What for?" Tanner challenged.

"Some of my cows are missing."

"So?"

"Found some cow tracks heading this way," Jeremiah said, and added, "Some horse tracks too."

"You accusing us of something?" Tanner narrowed his eyes.

"Depends."

"On what?"

"On what I find," Jeremiah replied. "Could be, some of your Pa's new hands got confused and drove my cattle over here by mistake."

"I think you're the one confused," Tanner sneered. "You'd best go home and drink some coffee."

Jeremiah looked at Tanner, and his hand rested on the butt of his Colt.

"I'll have a look at your cows," he said, and he nudged his horse forward.

5

"You will not!" Tanner warned.

Jeremiah ignored him as he rode on.

Tanner was furious, and he swung his rifle up.

Jeremiah made an attempt to grab his Colt. In his haste he mishandled his six-shooter, and before he could recover Tanner shot him out of the saddle.

As Jeremiah fell he grasped his Colt, and when he hit the ground he tried to raise up.

Tanner fired again, and Jeremiah's body was flipped over backwards. He kicked out and made some gurgling sounds as he died.

The sounds of the shots were loud. Ike Nash came running out of the house, and Butch Nelson was behind him.

"What's going on?" Ike demanded. "Who is that?" He pointed.

Tanner grinned and told him.

"You idiot!" Ike growled. "I told you to take his cows, not kill him!"

"You wanted his ranch," Tanner replied arrogantly. "Well, now you've got it."

Without warning, Ike struck Tanner a hard blow with the back of his hand.

Tanner hit the ground hard. His upper lip was busted, and he wiped the blood away with his sleeve as he glared up at his father.

"You'll never learn," Ike muttered.

Tanner didn't reply, and it was silent as Ike thought on the situation.

"You and a couple others take Jeremiah a long ways from here and bury him," Ike finally said. "Bury him deep, you hear?"

Tanner nodded sullenly as he got to his feet, and Ike glanced around at everyone.

6

"Everybody's to forget this happened," he raised his voice. "I don't want anybody talking about this. Understood?"

Everyone nodded.

Ike grunted, satisfied, and then he looked back at his son.

Tanner was just standing there with a sour look, and Ike frowned and mumbled something under his breath as he turned and walked back to the house.

Butch Nelson lingered. He chuckled softly at Tanner, and then he followed after Ike.

Tanner narrowed his eyes as he watched Butch. As soon as they were gone, he took charge.

"You," he pointed to two ranch hands named Rory Wheeler and Brock Jackson. "Throw him over a horse, and let's git."

Rory glanced uncertainly at Brock, but they still did as they were told.

Chapter one

Law in Empty-lake had once been Lieutenant Porter. But he was a bad man, so I killed him.

Soon after that Governor Davis sent out a new batch of policemen, and this bunch was mostly honest. I also had a pardon from Judge Parker, so they left me alone.

But mostly, the police force in Texas was corrupt, just like the Governor.

They were supposed to fight crime and help with frontier defense, but in most towns that didn't happen. Instead, Governor Davis used his police force to arrest anyone that opposed him.

But that all came to an end when Richard Coke defeated Governor Davis in 1874. Davis lost in a landslide, 85,549 to 42,663, and so ended the police force in Texas.

After that, law went back to the way it used to be. Towns elected sheriffs, and there was also talk that the Texas Rangers might get organized again.

So far Empty-lake hadn't elected a sheriff. So, when I saw the town council riding out to Mr. Tomlin's ranch headquarters one evening, I had a good idea what they were after.

My name is Rondo Landon.

I used to be a well-known outlaw, and I was also known as the man who killed Ben Kinrich. I wasn't proud of that, but it had to be done.

I was smaller than most, and my hips were narrow and my shoulders were wide. I was also in good shape on account of all the hard work at Mr. Tomlin's ranch.

For the past two years I had been an honest ranch hand. And, the only time I'd had to use my well-known white, ivory handled Colt was when my cousin Yancy needed some help over in the New Mexico Territory.

It had been a good two years.

8

Rachel and I had grown close, and marriage was on my mind. Problem was, I had nothing to offer.

I was down at the barn doing chores when they rode in, and I recognized all three.

Morgan McCann was tall and wide shouldered. He owned the local saloon.

Dave White owned the general store. He was an older man with white hair and stooped shoulders.

Fred Stilwell was the youngest. He was a businessman; he owned the bank.

They dismounted in front of the house. I heard them talking to Mr. Tomlin, and then they came down to the barn.

Even though I'd been pardoned, most folks were still uncomfortable being around me. In fact, the only folks that treated me normal were the Tomlins, Ross, and Jeremiah Batch.

They glanced uncertainly at each other, and then Fred Stilwell cleared his throat.

"Good evening, Mr. Landon," he said.

"Call me Rondo," I corrected.

"Yes, Mr. Landon," Fred said, and added, "I mean, Rondo."

I nodded and smiled.

"We've come to make you an offer," he announced. "We'd like you to be our sheriff."

"Why me?" I asked.

"We need someone with your, ah, qualifications."

"You mean someone that can use a gun," I replied.

"Yes, that is the qualification we were referring to," Fred smiled timidly.

I knew there was someone else who wanted the job, so I already had my answer.

"I appreciate the offer, but there's another more qualified," I said.

"Who?" Fred asked, surprised.

"Ross Stewart," I explained. "I might be better with a Colt, but I don't know much when it comes to the law. Ross is better educated than I am. I think he's the man you should talk to."

They glanced at each other and looked back at me.

"We discussed Ross, and we like him," Fred said. "But, we'd rather have you."

"Why?" I asked.

"Do you know who Ike Nash is?"

"I've heard of him."

"He showed up a few months ago with a lot of money, and he's been buying ranches all over Texas," Dave spoke up. "He has a lot of ranch hands, and they come to town every weekend. They tear up the saloon, take supplies from my store without paying for them, and scare honest folks."

"Last week one of them ran over a child in the street a-horseback, and he didn't even stop!" Fred added.

"Who was it?" I asked, concerned.

"My son," Morgan said, and there was anger in his voice.

"Is he all right?"

"He broke his foot and some ribs," Morgan said. "Doc says he might have a limp for the rest of his life."

"I'm sorry to hear that."

"It's got to stop," Fred spoke back up. "That's why we want you."

"Sounds more like you want my reputation," I said.

"I guess you could say that," Fred agreed.

"How many hands?" I asked.

"That come to town?" Fred asked. "Fifteen, sometimes twenty."

"Are they gun-hands, or cow-punchers?"

"They all carry guns," Fred replied.

I smiled at that.

"Any man can carry a gun, but that doesn't make 'em a gun-hand," I explained.

10

"I'll explain it this way," Morgan spoke up. "Ike has enough hands to run several ranches, yet he only has a small herd."

"So he's hiring gunmen," I said, and all three nodded.

I frowned at that and asked, "Would I get a deputy?"

"Why sure," Fred said. "You can even pick your own man."

"Tell him about the house, Fred," Dave said.

"House?" I asked.

"There's a little house on the edge of town that comes with the job," Fred explained.

"It'd be perfect for a man with, say, a wife," Dave said.

"Maybe even kids too, later on," Fred added helpfully.

I was embarrassed, and I felt my cheeks turning red.

They must have noticed my discomfort, because suddenly they all became very interested in the ground.

"Let me think on it," I said. "Give you my answer tomorrow."

They agreed, and they went over to their horses and mounted up.

I watched them leave, and then I went to find Ross.

Chapter two

Ross and I sat on the steps of the bunkhouse. It was almost dark, and we watched the sunset.

Ross had a tall and lanky frame, with tanned skin and brown hair. When he spoke he always displayed a rich, Texan drawl.

Ross was the curious sort, and he was always trying to solve some riddle. In fact, he even had suspicions about me when we first met, and he wasn't satisfied until he finally figured out who I really was.

His face was emotionless while I told him about the job offer. Afterwards, he pulled out a plug of tobacco, took a big bite, and spat as he thought on it.

"I was sorta hoping for the sheriff's job myself," he admitted.

"I know you was," I said.

Ross didn't reply, and I sighed.

"It seems we've always wanted the same things," I said.

"You're talking about Rachel now," Ross smiled faintly.

"I am."

"Well, you got her; we both know that," Ross said. "And, now it looks like you'll be sheriff."

"I told them I would think about it."

"You don't want the job?" Ross shot me a surprised look.

"To be honest, I'd rather stay here and punch cows," I said. "But, the sheriff's job comes with a house."

"For you and Rachel?"

"After we're married, of course," I nodded.

"You ask her yet?"

"How can I?" I replied. "Up 'til now I haven't had anything to offer. After all, we can't all live in the bunkhouse."

"No, I reckon not," Ross smiled.

12

"There's something else," I continued. "I get to pick my own deputy."

"Oh?"

"I can't think of nobody else I'd rather have than you."

"Deputy? Me?"

"I know it's not what you wanted," I said.

Ross didn't reply. He turned and watched the sunset, and his face was thoughtful.

"I never thought about being a deputy," he said. "I was sorta aiming for something higher."

"I need you, Ross," I said. "You know the law. I don't."

Ross nodded slowly, and he spit out another stream of tobacco.

"If we weren't friends," he declared, "I don't think I'd like you much."

I tried to smile, and Ross chuckled gruffly.

"I'm sorry, Ross," I said earnestly. "I really am."

"Aw, it ain't your fault," he waved his hand at me.

"So you'll be my deputy?"

"Somebody's gotta take care of you," Ross grumbled. "Might as well be me."

"Thanks, Ross," I said, relieved.

"Do you play chess?" He asked suddenly.

"No, never have."

"You're going to learn," Ross declared. "And then, I'm going to beat you. It's about time I beat you at something."

I chuckled as I stood.

"Sure, Ross, you can teach me."

He grunted in response.

"Well, reckon I'll go tell Mr. Tomlin," I said, and asked, "Want me to tell him you're going to be my deputy?"

"Might as well."

I nodded and left.

13

Chapter three

After chores, my daily routine was to go up to the main house and spend time with Rachel. Sometimes we would go for a walk; other times we would sit out on the front porch.

Mr. Tomlin was in his usual position. He was sitting in his chair by the front door, and he gave me a curious look as I walked up.

"You're late," he said. "Rachel's inside, waiting for you."

"I'd like to talk to you first, sir," I replied.

"Sit down," he offered, so I did.

Mr. Tomlin had white hair, and his face was weathered and wrinkled. But his eyes were thoughtful and sharp, and he never missed a thing.

It was silent as I gathered my thoughts, and then I cleared my throat.

"The town council offered me the sheriff's job," I announced.

"I figured they did," Mr. Tomlin replied, and added, "I'd hate to see you leave, but the decision is yours to make."

"There's nowhere else I'd rather be than here, sir," I said. "But, it's complicated."

"How so?"

"The job comes with a house."

"And why do you need a house?"

I felt my face getting red.

"Well," I squirmed. "I would need a house, sir, if I was to get married."

Mr. Tomlin didn't say anything, and his face was blank. I suddenly became very interested in the floor.

"Are you asking for my daughter's hand?" He finally asked.

14

"Well, not right away, but it's been on my mind," I replied. "That's the only reason I'm considering taking the job. After all, a married couple has to have a place to live."

"It helps," he agreed.

"And that ain't all," I said. "Ross has agreed to become my deputy."

"Well! You're just full of news," Mr. Tomlin looked startled. "So, I'm losing my two best hands?"

"I haven't accepted the job yet."

"But you will," Mr. Tomlin smiled. "Especially if you want to marry my daughter."

I was startled.

"I have your permission?" I asked.

"When the time comes," Mr. Tomlin nodded, "you have my permission."

A grin spread across my face. Before I could reply, Rachel appeared at the door.

"There you are," she scolded playfully. "Where have you been?"

"I've been talking to your father," I explained.

"About what?"

I hesitated. I glanced at Mr. Tomlin for help, but he just smiled and stood.

"I'm turning in," he announced. "You two have a lot to talk about."

He hugged Rachel and went inside, and it was silent and awkward while Rachel waited for me to say something.

Rachel had long, brown hair with sandy looking freckles that covered her face. She also had a knowing smile that always made me squirm, and she was giving me that look now.

"So, what do we have to discuss?" She finally urged.

Suddenly, I became very interested in the floor again.

15

Chapter four

It took a while, but I finally told Rachel about the job offer. Afterwards, she was silent as she thought on it.

"Is this what you want?" She asked.

"Not really," I admitted. "I like punching cows better."

"Then why accept?"

I told her about the house.

"And why is a house so important?" She asked.

My heart started thumping, and suddenly I didn't know what to do with my hands. I crossed my arms, and then uncrossed them. Meanwhile, Rachel looked slightly amused as she watched me.

"Well," I hesitated. "I figure a married couple needs a house."

It was now out in the open, and I held my breath as I watched her.

Rachel looked surprised. A grin spread across her face, and my heart skipped a beat.

"Is this a proposal?"

"Uh, no, not yet," I stammered. "It's more like a promise *of* a proposal."

Rachel didn't say anything, but the grin on her face told me all that I needed to know.

I smiled as I turned and looked out into the night. It was silent for a while, and then I cleared my throat.

"There is one reason I hesitate to take the job," I said.

"Oh?"

"Killing is a-," I paused while I searched for the right words, "-killing is a by-product of being sheriff. Sooner or later, it'll happen."

"And that bothers you?" Rachel asked, and her eyes were wide and alert as she watched me.

"It does," I admitted. "I've never told you, but there's a feeling that runs deep inside of me."

"What sort of feeling?"

"A killing feeling," I explained. "Yancy and Cooper have felt it too. It's a feeling of pure meanness."

"And you don't like this feeling?"

"I don't like killing people," I replied. "It stays with me for a long time. Even the bad ones. And, I'm afraid if I kill too many I'll snap just like Ben Kinrich did."

"You are nothing like Ben Kinrich," Rachel retorted. "You are kind and have a gentle heart. Kinrich was a cold-hearted killer with no morals."

"He wasn't like that in the beginning," I reminded. "He changed over time. Each time he killed somebody, he changed just a little bit."

"Well you won't," Rachel declared.

I smiled, and it fell silent as we thought our own thoughts.

"With you living in town, we won't get to see each other every day," Rachel said after a while.

"I know," I frowned.

Rachel sighed. She looked up at the stars, and then she glanced at me.

"I'll miss this," she said wistfully.

"So will I," I nodded, and added, "If things work out, soon we'll be able to spend every evening together."

"That would be nice," Rachel smiled.

Chapter five

The next morning I saddled Desperate and trotted into town.

I pulled up in front of the sheriff's office, and I smiled as I remembered back.

Lieutenant Porter had built the sheriff's office with his corrupt tax money. And, it was still the fanciest building in town. There were living quarters in a side room beside the office, and in the back were six well-built cells. There was a thick wall dividing the cells from the front rooms, and there was also a front porch with windows that lined the front.

The three members of the town council walked up as I dismounted.

"Morning," I said.

"Good morning, Mr. Landon," Fred said, and added, "I mean, Rondo."

I smiled pleasantly.

"Shall we go inside?" Fred offered.

I nodded, and we walked in. I sat behind the desk, and Fred sat across from me. Dave and Morgan remained standing.

"Have you made a decision?" Fred asked.

"Why I'm here," I said. "I've decided to accept."

They looked pleased, and they glanced at each other and smiled.

"I want Ross as my deputy," I said.

"That's fine, just fine," Fred agreed.

"Good," I said, and added, "So, what's next?"

They glanced uncertainly at each other.

"I'm not quite sure," Fred admitted. "We've never hired a sheriff before."

"I see," I scratched my jaw. "Well, seems like I should be sworn in. Anybody know the words?"

They glanced at each other and shook their heads.

"I'll make some up," Fred offered.

Nobody said anything, so Fred turned to me.

"You swear to protect this town to the best of your abilities?"

"I do," I nodded.

"Then you're the sheriff," Fred declared, and Dave and Morgan nodded in agreement.

"I accept," I smiled, and then asked, "When does Ike Nash's hands come to town?"

"Usually on Friday night," Morgan spoke up.

"Today's Thursday, so that only gives me a day to get settled," I figured, and then I stood. "Well, if you'll excuse me, I'd like to take a look at the house."

They nodded as I walked to the door.

I started to walk out, but Fred stopped me. He walked behind the desk, opened the drawer, and grabbed something.

"Aren't you forgetting this?" He tossed me a badge.

I smiled sheepishly as I caught it, and then I pinned the badge on.

"How does it look?" I asked.

"Fine, just fine," Fred said, and Dave and Morgan agreed.

I turned and looked at my reflection in the window.

The badge was displayed in full view on my vest pocket, and I couldn't help but smile.

"It does, doesn't it?" I said.

Chapter six

The house was small and simple and needed painting. But it still looked mighty good to me.

There was a porch, a kitchen, a front room, and two bedrooms.

There were cobwebs in the corners, and the place needed a good sweeping. But I could handle that.

I walked out the front door, and I smiled as I pictured Rachel standing in the doorway, wearing an apron covered in flour, waving me off to work.

I was still standing there, deep in thought, when I heard a movement from behind. I also smelled cigar smoke.

"Well, hello there, Button," a rich, southern voice drawled.

I turned around, and Lee Mattingly and Brian Clark stood in the street.

I knew them well. Both were outlaws, just like I had been.

Lee Mattingly was in his mid-thirties.

During the war he had been a loyal soldier for the South, and then he drifted out west and joined up with Ben Kinrich. After that, he rode with the Oltman brothers.

Lee had a gentlemen like way about him. And, he also had a different set of ethics than most outlaws. He was soft spoken, and he was loyal to those that he considered friends.

As for Brian, he was in his mid-fifties. He was a grizzled veteran, and he was wanted in nearly every territory or state there was.

Like Lee, Brian also had a gentle-like way about him. He was always careful; he never took any chances unless he had to.

Over the past few years, an unspoken friendship had sprouted between Lee and me. There was always a struggle

20

going on inside Lee between right and wrong, and I knew all too well how that felt.

Lee's eyes twinkled as he studied me, but then his eyes grew wide when he noticed my sheriff's badge.

"Is that what I think it is?"

"Yep. I'm the sheriff," I announced.

Lee's mouth fell open. He glanced at Brian and looked back at me.

"You, a lawman? I don't believe it."

"It's true," I smiled.

It was silent as they thought on that. Lee shook his head, and then he glanced at the house.

"This your house?"

"Sure is," I announced with pride.

"We just rode into town. Mind some company?"

"For how long?" I asked suspiciously.

"Just until we get settled."

"Settled?" I frowned. "Long as I've known you, you've never settled anywhere."

"Well, we're settling now," Lee said as they pushed by me and entered the house.

"It's a bit dusty," I protested as I followed after them.

"That doesn't matter to us," Lee said as he looked around. "Nice place! What room do you want?"

I pointed, and they stowed their belongings in the other bedroom.

I frowned as I watched them.

I had sorta wanted to be alone; that way I could fix up the house. But, I figured a few days wouldn't matter.

"Is that café down the street any good?" Lee wanted to know.

"Sure."

"Buy you lunch," Lee offered, and I nodded.

21

Chapter seven

A few minutes later we were sitting at a table in the café. We ordered coffee, beans, and steak.

The café was a long, narrow room. There were a few windows, and there was also an old piano in the back corner. It wasn't fancy, but the food was good, and that's all that mattered.

Fred had arranged for me to have free meals, so I figured I'd quickly become a regular.

"What is this you said about settling down?" I asked while we waited for our food.

"I've decided to take your advice and quit the outlaw business," Lee announced, and Brian nodded. "From here on out, we're going to be respectable business men."

I didn't believe him, and I frowned suspiciously.

"Doing what?"

"We're here to build a hotel," Lee announced.

"Hotel?"

"Yep. Fanciest hotel Texas has ever seen," Lee said. "It's going to have a restaurant and a real nice poker room. Brian will run things while I handle the poker room."

"We've already bought the land and hired a crew to build the place," Brian added. "They should be here soon."

I was speechless as I stared at them.

"Hotel," I said again.

"That's right," they nodded.

"That's going to take money," I said.

"We've plenty of that," Lee waved his hand at me.

"And I can imagine how you got it," I frowned disapprovingly.

"You'd be wrong," Lee corrected. "We earned it honest."

"Since I'm sheriff, would you mind telling me how?"

Lee glanced at Brian. He nodded, so Lee turned back to me.

"Some of the money is ours, but we've also got a partner," he explained.

"Who?"

"She wants to remain a silent partner."

"She?"

Lee's eyes grew wide, and Brian sighed.

"You weren't supposed to know that," Lee grumbled.

"I won't tell," I smiled, and added, "Whoever she is, she must trust you two."

"She does," Lee declared. "And, we ain't gonna let her down neither."

The waiter brought our food, and it was silent while we ate. Afterwards, I frowned as I thought on it.

"Your hotel will bring in a lot of business," I figured.

"That's what we're hoping," Lee said.

"That'll make my job more difficult," I pointed out.

"Think you can handle it?" Lee asked.

"We'll see," I said, and then I chuckled.

"What's so funny?" Lee wanted to know.

"Wait until Yancy hears about this," I said. "He'll never believe it."

"Yancy's still trying to figure out how Stew Baine was killed," Lee grinned.

"Didn't Sergeant Wagons kill him?" I asked, confused.

Brian chuckled, and Lee's eyes twinkled.

"Sure," Lee said.

Chapter eight

For two years now, I had been saving up some money for a wedding ring.

The money was stashed in my saddlebags. After lunch I went and dug it out, and then I walked over to the general store.

It seemed like every lady in town was there. I hung in the back, but then Dave spotted me.

"Help you, Sheriff?" He asked.

I nodded and walked over.

"I'm looking for something," I said.

Suddenly, the room was very quiet.

"Looking for what?" Dave prompted.

I glanced sideways at the ladies, and then I lowered my voice.

"Wedding rings," I whispered.

"Say what?" Dave held his hand up to his ear.

"Wedding rings," I said louder, and everyone in the room heard me.

"Oh, that!" Dave said.

My face turned red while all the ladies smiled at each other. Meanwhile, Dave dug around in the back, and he brought me a tray lined with rings.

I looked them over. They all looked the same to me, and I frowned in confusion.

"Which one do you think Rachel would like?" I asked.

"You can probably afford this one," Dave pointed one out.

"I'll take it," I said.

***

I paid for the ring and went back to the jail. I sat at my desk, and I took the ring out and looked it over. A grin spread across my face as I pictured Rachel wearing it.

I was still daydreaming when I heard a noise at the door. I looked up and spotted Lee and Brian.

Lee grinned when he spotted the ring.

"Is that for Rachel?"

"Yes," I admitted with a sheepish grin.

"You ask her yet?"

"If I had, she would be wearing this ring," I pointed out.

"Unless she said no," Lee's eyes twinkled.

"When the time comes, she'll say yes," I declared.

Lee chuckled as I put the ring away.

"When are you going to ask her?" He asked.

"I'll get around to it," I replied.

"Don't wait too long," he cautioned me. "She might get tired of waiting and marry someone else."

I frowned and grunted in response.

Chapter nine

I rode out to the ranch that afternoon.

Ross and I packed our belongings, and then we went up to the main house to eat supper with the Tomlins.

For some reason, I was nervous around Rachel. I now had a house and a ring, and the next step was to ask her to marry me. I suddenly realized that asking her might be tougher than I had thought.

We were early, and while we waited Ross taught me the basics of chess. He showed me how each piece moved, and we played a quick game. He won easily.

"Complicated game," I frowned as we sat around the dinner table.

"It takes time to understand," Ross explained.

"I think I like poker better," I grumbled.

"But I can't beat you at poker," Ross reminded. "Besides, anybody can play poker. But it takes years to become a strong chess player."

"Poker ain't easy either," I argued. "It takes a lot of practice."

"Isn't," Rachel corrected with a smile.

"Yeah," I nodded emphatically. "That too."

***

After supper I said goodbye to Rachel, and then Ross and I mounted up. While we trotted to town I told Ross about Morgan's son getting ran over in the street.

"What can we do about that?" I asked.

"Well," Ross looked thoughtful. "We could arrest him for attempted murder."

"And then what?"

"We'd have to send for Judge Parker and hold a trial."

"And then?" I pressed.

26

"If convicted, he'd be sent to prison for however long Judge Parker sentenced him."

I grunted in approval and nodded.

"Are you sure you want to go that far?" Ross asked with a concerned look. "Might stir up trouble. Be more peaceful if we gave them a stern warning first."

"No," I shook my head. "I want to come down hard. We let 'em know now that our intentions are serious, and mebbe there won't be anymore trouble."

"He won't be alone when we arrest him," Ross warned.

"I'm sure he won't," I agreed.

Ross looked concerned, but he didn't say anything else. We rode a bit further, and then he changed the subject.

"I know you're planning on getting married and all, but would it be all right if I stayed with you for a while?" He asked.

I hesitated, and then I explained about Lee and Brian.

"I won't take up much room," Ross replied.

I frowned as I thought on it.

"Well, I reckon you can," I finally said, and added, "For now."

Ross smiled and nodded, and then he chuckled.

"So, the first thing you did as sheriff was to invite two famous outlaws to board with you," he pointed out.

"They sorta invited themselves, but I reckon you could say that."

"This should be fun, all us staying together," Ross looked pleased.

"For now," I said again.

27

Chapter ten

The next morning I cooked breakfast for my three boarders.

Afterwards, Lee and Brian hurried off to start planning their hotel. I cleaned up the dishes, and then Ross and I went down to the jail.

Ross made some coffee, and we sat out on the front porch and watched the activity on the street. It was shady and cool, and we had a good view.

As we sat there folks stopped and welcomed us and exchanged pleasantries. Almost everyone looked relieved to have a sheriff, and several mentioned that I was the perfect man for the job.

Hearing that made me feel good. However, I could also tell that it bothered Ross just a bit.

A few hours passed, but we were in no hurry. We drank another pot of coffee, and it was then that I noticed a rider coming into town.

I can't explain why, but there was just something about him that made me look again. He was an older man, probably in his sixties, and he sat up very straight in the saddle.

There was something familiar about him, but I couldn't place what it was. He had a smaller build, and he looked to be spry and collected. I also noticed that he displayed a black handled Colt on his hip.

I straightened up in my chair, and my gun hand hovered naturally over my Colt.

Ross noticed my movements, and he turned and looked down the street.

"Somebody's coming into town," he commented.

"Recognize him?" I asked.

"Nope," Ross shook his head.

The stranger spotted us and rode over. He pulled up, and it was silent while we studied each other.

28

There was a professional carefulness in his eyes. It was a look I knew all too well.

"Just got into town," he said in a soft, clear voice. "You the sheriff?"

"I am," I nodded and beckoned at Ross. "Ross is my deputy."

He nodded as he looked up the street, and then he glanced back at me.

"I'm here to kill a man," he announced. "Figured you should know."

I was startled. I glanced at Ross and looked back at the stranger.

"It'll be a fair fight when it happens," he added.

"I can't let you just ride into town and kill somebody," I protested.

"It won't happen for a while. I plan to get a room and rest up for a few days," he said, and he looked me straight in the eyes. "I'd advise you not to get in my way."

I met his look, and it was silent for a long time. Neither one of us wavered.

"Who exactly are you here to kill?" I finally asked. "You can at least tell me that."

"I suppose I can," he agreed, and then he announced, "I'm here to kill Rondo Landon."

A surprised jolt passed through me. I glanced at Ross again and cleared my throat.

"Why?" I asked.

"I have my reasons."

"I'd sure like to hear them," I said.

"Why is it your concern?"

"Because I'm Rondo Landon," I announced.

A small glimpse of surprise showed in his eyes, but that was all. He studied me carefully and nodded to himself.

"I should have known," he said softly. "You fit the description."

"I don't know why you feel the need to kill me, but I'm sure we can talk about this," I said.

"Too late for that."

"But I don't even know who you are," I protested.

"The name's Virgil," he said. "Virgil Carson."

"And why do you want to kill me?"

"I just got into town," he replied. "There'll be time for explanations later."

I frowned at that but didn't reply.

Virgil nodded at us, and he kicked up his horse and went on down the street.

I watched him leave, and then I turned to Ross.

"What was that all about?" Ross asked.

"I have no idea," I replied.

"What do you think?"

I listened to the question, and it was silent as I thought on it.

"I think he's dangerous," I finally replied. "*Very* dangerous."

Chapter eleven

That afternoon Ross and I took a stroll and better familiarized ourselves with the town.

"What are we going to do about Virgil?" Ross asked as we headed back toward the jail.

"Not sure yet," I replied.

"Figured out why he wants to kill you?"

"No."

"Mebbe you and Kinrich stole something from him," Ross reasoned.

"I don't think so," I said. "He's a gunfighter; not a rancher or farmer. And, if we did rob him, he wouldn't wait this long to come after me."

"Mebbe he wants to be known as the man who killed Rondo Landon," Ross suggested.

"He doesn't seem to be a glory hunter," I disagreed, and added, "We'll worry about him later. Right now, we need to focus on tonight."

"It is Friday, ain't it."

"It is."

"Do you think Ike's hands will come to town tonight?"

"Morgan said they usually do."

"And what are we going to do?" Ross asked.

"Keep the peace," I said, and added, "If he shows up, we'll also arrest the feller that ran over Morgan's son."

"How will we know him?"

"Morgan said he was tall, thin, and had a noticeable scar across his cheek."

Ross nodded as he thought on that.

"Be dark soon," I glanced at the sun. "We'd best get something to eat. Might be a long night."

We arrived at the jail. Ross cooked up some supper, and we played a game of chess while we ate. Again, Ross won easily.

31

We played a few more games, and then I heard a noise at the door.

In one motion I drew my Colt and spun around.

It was Lee and Brian. They were startled, and they held their hands up.

"Don't shoot!" Lee exclaimed.

"Sorry," I smiled sheepishly as I holstered my Colt, and then I asked, "How's the hotel business?"

"We'll be ready to start building Monday morning," Brian said.

"Good," I said.

It was silent for a moment, and I noticed that Lee was watching me with a curious look.

"Why are you so jumpy?" He asked.

I explained about Virgil Carson and the trouble with Ike Nash's hands. Afterwards, Lee scratched his jaw as he thought on everything.

"Well now. That's interesting," he said.

"I knew you were going to say that," I smiled, and asked, "Have you ever heard of Virgil Carson?"

"No," both Lee and Brian shook their heads, and then Lee asked, "Is he good with a gun?"

"He's still alive, so I reckon he's been good enough," I said.

Lee frowned thoughtfully. He started to say something, but before he could there were loud noises from the street. Whooping and shooting sounded out, and we could hear several horses loping down the street.

"Well," Lee said wryly, "sounds like they're here."

Chapter twelve

Ike Nash's hands rode up in front of Morgan's saloon and dismounted. They tied their horses to the hitching rail and marched inside.

Tanner wasn't with them.

Ike was still upset with his son, and he had him doing chores at the ranch. So, a man with a scar across his cheek led the way as they lined up at the bar.

Butch Nelson was also with them, but he held back.

Butch was a plain looking man. Short with a broad face, he looked more like a storekeeper.

But he was far from that. He was very good with a Colt, and he displayed one on his hip. However, even with the Colt, there was still nothing that really stood out. And, that's how Butch preferred it.

Morgan's saloon was simple but nice. There was a mahogany bar that lined down one side, and in the middle were a few tables. Behind that was the poker room.

Everyone demanded a drink of whiskey. Morgan was behind the bar, and he frowned hesitantly.

"I'd like to discuss your bill first," he said.

"Later," the man with the scar laughed, and he shoved Morgan backwards. He reached behind the bar, grabbed a few bottles of whiskey, and slid them down to his companions.

Nobody took the time to grab a glass. Instead, they drank it straight from the bottle.

Butch watched them, and there was a hint of disgust in his eyes. He grabbed a bottle and a glass, and then he looked around the room.

Most of the town folks were leaving.

However, sitting at a corner table, there was an older man shuffling a deck of cards that paid them no attention.

33

Butch narrowed his eyes as he studied the man. Finally, he nodded to himself and walked over.

The older man took a swig of coffee as Butch stopped in front of him. He carefully wiped his mouth with a napkin and looked up at Butch.

Several seconds passed, and then he cleared his throat.

"You looking for something?" He asked in a clear, soft voice.

"You're Virgil Carson," Butch said.

A hint of surprise showed in his face.

"I am," he said, and added, "Who are you?"

"Butch Nelson."

"I've heard that name," Virgil said.

"Not many have."

"You ain't much to look at," Virgil observed. "But if what I've heard is true, then you're a dangerous man."

"As are you," Butch said, and asked, "Can I join you?"

"Go ahead."

Butch nodded and sat.

He poured a drink while Virgil studied the men at the bar. They were still loud and carrying on.

"Those your men?" Virgil asked, and there was a disapproving look in his eyes.

"Nope," Butch replied. "They work for Ike Nash, and so do I."

"I've heard of Ike," Virgil replied. "He was mixed up with Governor Davis but escaped punishment, and now he's one of the richest men in Texas. I've also heard he's involved in several businesses."

"You heard right."

"Why are you working for him?"

"Gotta work for somebody," Butch shrugged. "Besides, Ike pays good."

Virgil nodded and changed the subject.

"How did you know who I was?" He asked.

"We once had a mutual friend."

34

"Oh?" Virgil raised an eyebrow. "Who?"

"Ben Kinrich."

Virgil was surprised, and he frowned at Butch.

"He mentioned me?"

"He was drunk," Butch explained. "In fact, he was so drunk he even admitted that you were faster with a Colt."

"I am," Virgil declared, and asked, "How much did he tell you?"

"He told me how the whole set-up worked," Butch said. "You planned everything, and then Ben and his men pulled the jobs."

"Ben never could hold his liquor," Virgil scowled.

"Well, your set-up worked great until Rondo Landon came along," Butch said.

"That's why I'm here."

"You're here for Rondo?" Butch asked, startled.

"I am."

"What I hear, he doesn't come to town very often," Butch warned.

"You don't know?" Virgil looked at him.

"Know what?"

"He's the sheriff."

Butch was surprised.

"It must have just happened," he said. "Last I heard, he was just a ranch hand."

"He ain't now."

"Ike will want to know about this," Butch said thoughtfully, and asked, "You already saw Rondo?"

"I did."

"And he's still alive?"

"I'm in no hurry."

Butch was curious, but he didn't say anything more. It fell silent, and then Virgil cleared his throat.

"Speaking of Rondo, he just walked through the door," he said.

Butch turned in his seat, looked, and nodded.

"Yeah, and that's Lee Mattingly behind him," he added.

Chapter thirteen

"How many?" I asked.

Lee walked over to the window and looked out.

"I count eighteen," he said.

"Is that all?" I smiled, and then I looked at Ross. "Ross, grab your shotgun. When we go in, I want you to stay at the door and cover everybody. Don't shoot unless you have to."

Ross nodded soberly as he grabbed his shotgun from the gun cabinet. We both checked our weapons, and then I looked at Lee and Brian.

"Be seeing you," I said.

Lee smiled and glanced at Brian.

"Want some coffee, Brian?"

"Sure," he nodded.

"So do I," Lee looked at me and grinned. "Think we'll come along."

"I ain't asking for help," I objected.

"You never do," Lee said. "And, I ain't offering. However, if bullets start flying around, I'll be obliged to defend myself."

I thought on that and nodded.

"Come on then," I said.

Lee's eyes twinkled as we stepped outside. Ross and I were in front, and Lee and Brian followed.

Concerned citizens stopped and watched us, and it was quite a sight as we made our way to the saloon.

It was then that the feeling came all over me. I felt alert, calm, and ready.

We stepped up onto the porch, and I glanced at Ross and nodded. He was nervous, but he managed to nod back.

"Here we go," I said softly, and we walked inside.

Chapter fourteen

It was dark, so I paused at the doorway and allowed my eyes to adjust. Then, I took a slow look around.

Most of the men were lined up at the bar, laughing and drinking. They had knocked over the spittoons, and there was broken glass on the floor.

Morgan was behind the bar, and he looked relieved to see me.

At a corner table sat Virgil Carson and another man. Virgil was watching me, and there was a hint of amusement in his eyes.

I took a deep breath and walked towards the bar. Ross stayed at the door, and Lee and Brian moved to my right and spread out.

A tall, slender man with a scar across his cheek was closest. I looked at Morgan, and he nodded slightly.

Scar-face sneered at me as I stopped in front of them.

"Who are you?" He asked.

"Name's Rondo Landon," I said. "I'm the sheriff. Fella behind me with the shotgun is my deputy, Ross."

"Sheriff!" Scar-face sneered, and the rest of the men laughed. "What do you want?"

"First thing; I want all of you to pay for past damages," I said. "You boys have run up quite a tab here, and you also owe Dave at the General store. I have a list."

They stared at me in disbelief, and then Scar-face laughed wolfishly.

"And if we don't?"

"Then I'll arrest you."

His face filled with scorn.

"What if we don't want to be arrested?" He asked.

"Then we'll shoot you," I said.

"All of us?"

"Depends."

"On what?"

"How good you all can shoot."

"You can't get all of us," Scar-face said.

"Probably not, but you'll be the first man I get," I said, and added, "Matter of fact, you're also under arrest for attempted murder. The rest of you can leave. You can't."

"You can't threaten me," Scar-face snarled.

"Actually, I can," I corrected. "I'm doing it now."

It fell silent. They glanced at each other, and then they looked back at me.

I kept my eyes on Scar-face. He looked uncertain, but then his face got hard.

His shoulder twitched, and I grabbed for my Colt. It was a smooth draw, and I had my Colt out before Scar-face even touched his handle.

I fired two shots into his midsection, and there was a loud thump as his body was flung backwards. He landed on several of his friends, and they all fell backwards.

It happened so suddenly that everyone else was frozen, and before they could react Ross pulled the hammer back on his shotgun. It made a loud click, and nobody knew what to do.

"Anyone else?" I asked tersely as I covered them with my Colt.

Before anybody could do anything, the man that was sitting with Virgil Carson stood.

"Everyone hold your fire," he said in a calm, stern voice.

"Who are you?" I asked as he walked over.

"Name's Butch Nelson."

"You the foreman?"

"You could say that," he said, and added, "We don't want anymore trouble. We'll leave peaceable."

"All right. You can take him with you," I gestured at Scar-face.

"Sure," Butch nodded.

"And the next time you boys come to town, everyone's to act peaceable and respectable. This is my town now, and I won't tolerate this sort of behavior," I said, and I reached into my pocket and pulled out a piece of paper. "This is a list of all the damages."

I handed the list to Butch, and he looked amused as he put it in his pocket.

"I'll give this to Mr. Nash," he said.

"Tell him he has a week to pay."

Butch nodded and glanced at his men.

"Somebody grab him," he gestured at Scar-face.

The men didn't like it, but they did as they were told.

Two of them picked up Scar-face, and then they all walked out the door. We heard them mounting up, and then they left town.

There was still a smoky smell of gunpowder in the room, and there was also some blood splattered on the floor.

While Morgan grabbed a mop, I reloaded and holstered my Colt. Then, I glanced at Ross.

"You all right?" I asked.

Ross still looked nervous, but he managed to smile and nod.

"I'm fine," he said.

"You can ease that hammer back down now," I suggested.

Ross smiled sheepishly and accommodated my request.

I smiled and looked at Lee. He didn't say anything, but I could tell that he was enjoying himself.

From the corner, Virgil Carson cleared his throat.

"You're mighty fast with that Colt," he said.

"I am," I agreed.

"You ruined my evening plans."

"How so?" I asked, confused.

"I was hoping for a game of poker, but you ran off all my potential competition," he explained.

"Tough luck," I said.

Virgil didn't reply as he looked at Lee.

"You'd be Lee Mattingly," he said.

"That's right," Lee nodded.

"I've heard of you," Virgil said, and added, "Care for a game of poker?"

"Why not?" Lee said.

"Rondo?" Virgil offered.

"No thanks," I shook my head. "I'll just watch a while."

Virgil looked disappointed.

"I hear you're quite good," he said.

"You hear a lot," I replied.

"I do," Virgil nodded.

I didn't reply as Lee and Brian sat at Virgil's table. Meanwhile, I grabbed a pot of coffee, and Ross and I sat behind them.

Lee cut the deck, and the game started.

Chapter fifteen

It was a somber ride back to the ranch.

Butch assigned a burial detail, and then he tended to his horse and went up to the main house.

Ike Nash was seated behind his desk, and he looked up curiously when Butch entered.

"Back so soon?" He asked.

Ike Nash was a big man. Deep voiced, wide shouldered, and tall, he had a commanding presence that made most folks uncomfortable.

Ike was a businessman. All he cared about was how to make a profit, and he was very shrewd and cunning.

He had been deeply involved with Governor Davis's schemes, but he also had good sense to get out before it caved on him. Since then, he'd been running things on his own. All across Texas he had created his own little empire, and he was just getting started.

He was also very good with a Colt. However, he kept this to himself, and even Butch didn't know how good he really was.

"We ran into a little problem," Butch said, and then he explained.

Ike listened carefully, and he nodded as he thought the situation over.

"Rondo Landon," he said thoughtfully. "I had thought about offering him a job. We could use a man like that."

"Maybe a few years ago, but not now," Butch said. "He seems to be taking the sheriff's job seriously."

"That's too bad," Ike frowned. "I need the sheriff to be on my side. It makes things easier."

"I could talk to him," Butch offered. "But, I don't think it would do any good."

"He needs to be replaced then."

"Replace him with who?" Butch asked, curious.

42

"How about you?" Ike suggested.

"Me? Sheriff?"

"Sure. You're good with a gun, could keep the peace, and also handle my affairs."

Butch frowned thoughtfully.

"Well, it's an idea."

"And a good idea too," Ike decided. "But first, we have to get rid of Rondo Landon."

"He has a deputy," Butch warned. "And, Lee Mattingly and Brian Clark are also in town."

"Lee Mattingly?" Ike looked intrigued. "Now there's a man I'd like to hire. Brian too."

"I don't think so," Butch disagreed. "He and Brian are in town to build a hotel. Seems like they want to become businessmen."

"Lee Mattingly, a businessman?" Ike raised an eyebrow.

"What I hear, they have the money," Butch said. "This hotel is supposed to be mighty fancy."

"Well, that's just fine," Ike said. "Let them build it. And then, when this hotel is finished, I'll take it from them. Then they'll be broke and might be more hirable."

"How will you take the hotel?"

"Men like them have weaknesses," Ike replied. "All we have to do is figure out what they are."

Butch thought on that and nodded.

"What about Rondo?" Butch changed the subject.

"I don't care how you do it, but get rid of him and his deputy," Ike said. "And remember; it can't come back to us. Make it look like we had nothing to do with it."

A thought occurred to Butch, and he snapped his fingers.

"We might not have to do anything at all," he said, and he explained about Virgil Carson.

Afterwards, Ike nodded thoughtfully.

"That might just work," Ike said. "And then, after he kills Rondo, you can run Virgil out of town."

43

"What for?" Butch looked confused.

"It'll make you look good in front of the town folks," Ike explained, and added, "That's what a sheriff does."

"Virgil's mighty handy with a Colt," Butch objected.

"Better than you?"

"I wouldn't say that. But he's good. Real good."

Ike thought on that and smiled.

"Maybe you could talk to Virgil," he suggested, "and offer to pay him to leave town peaceful?"

"I'll do that," Butch nodded.

"Good," Ike said, and added, "And tell the boys to behave themselves. I don't want anymore trouble until this is taken care of."

"I'll tell them," Butch said, and then he reached into his pocket. "I almost forgot. I'm supposed to give you this."

"What is it?" Ike asked as Butch handed him a piece of paper.

"This is a list of damages," Butch explained. "Rondo said you have a week."

Ike grunted and chuckled wolfishly.

Chapter sixteen

It didn't take Morgan long to clean the place up.

Most of the blood had splattered on Scar-face's friends, so there wasn't much for him to mop up.

He swept up the broken glass and picked up the spittoons, and things returned to normal. Some of the town folks eased back in, and a few of them even joined the poker game.

Ross and I drank coffee and watched, and it didn't take me long to figure out that Virgil was an exceptional poker player.

It took everyone else a bit longer. After an hour Lee was the biggest loser, and Brian wasn't that far behind.

I could tell that Lee was getting frustrated, but he didn't say anything.

As I watched Virgil deal the cards, it suddenly occurred to me who he reminded me of. But it didn't make any sense, and I frowned thoughtfully.

By the second hour the town folks had had enough. They left, and then it was just Lee, Brian, and Virgil.

Virgil was still winning most of the hands, and the pots kept getting higher.

"I think it's time we called it a night," Brian finally said.

"No," Lee declared. "We'll play a little longer."

Brian frowned, but didn't say anything.

The game continued, and I could tell that Lee thought he finally had a good hand. He bet big. Brian folded, but Virgil matched the pot.

"Three kings," Lee announced with a smile.

Virgil nodded and laid down his cards.

"Four nines," he said softly.

Lee snorted in disgust.

"No man gets this lucky," he grumbled. "You've been playing us all night."

45

"Lee," Brian warned, but Lee ignored him.

Virgil didn't say anything as he leaned forward and collected his winnings. His face was emotionless as he stared at Lee.

"You accusing me of something?" Virgil asked in a soft and clear voice.

"No man gets this lucky," Lee repeated.

The room was suddenly very quiet. Both Virgil and Lee straightened up in their chairs, trying to get ready.

"You'd better take back that remark," Virgil said.

Lee didn't reply. They just stared at each other, and the silence was tense.

"Sheriff," Virgil said, and his eyes never left Lee's. "You think I was cheating?"

I pinched my face in thought, and then I sighed.

"No," I said truthfully. "I don't think you were."

"You're sure?" Lee asked as he stared at Virgil.

"If I thought he was cheating, I would have already said something," I said.

Lee nodded, and his stare softened.

"Rondo's word is good enough for me," he told Virgil. "I take it back."

Virgil nodded. He pocketed his winnings, stood, and looked at me.

"I'm calling it a evening," he said, and added, "I'll see you later."

"Thanks for the warning," I said.

Virgil's face remained emotionless. He scooted his chair back and walked toward the door.

Soon as he was gone, Lee exhaled loudly.

"How much did you lose?" I asked.

"Enough," Lee grumbled.

"Enough to hurt your hotel?"

Lee thought for a moment.

"No," he said. "But, I might have to quit eating steak and live on beans for a while."

"Not if you're staying with me," I smiled. It was silent for a moment, and I asked Lee, "Virgil remind you of anybody?"

"Should he?"

"I've only seen one other feller besides me that deals cards like that," I said. "He also rides a horse like him, walks like him, and wears a Colt like him."

"Who?" Lee wanted to know.

"Ben Kinrich," I announced.

Lee and Brian were startled. They looked at each other and then looked at me.

"You're right," Brian agreed. "I'm surprised I didn't notice it before."

"You reckon Virgil is Ben's pappy?" Lee asked. "He'd be the right age."

"No, Ben's folks were killed by Comanches when he was a youngster," I reminded.

"Then who is he?"

"I don't know," I said, and added, "But I'm going to find out."

It was silent as we all thought on that, and then Ross cleared his throat.

"Whoever he is, he sure has a dry personality," he said.

"Does," I agreed.

"Mebbe he wasn't hugged enough as a kid," Ross suggested.

"Mebbe so," I smiled.

Chapter seventeen

The next morning we all went down to the jail. I made some coffee, and we sat out on the front porch.

Lee was in a grumpy mood. He was still upset about the poker game, and soon as he finished his coffee he and Brian left to buy some building supplies for their hotel. Meanwhile, I made another pot of coffee, and Ross and I watched the activity in the street.

"Busy night last night," Ross commented.

"It was," I agreed.

"What do you suppose will happen now?" Ross asked, and added, "With Ike Nash's hands, I mean."

"Not sure."

"Think they'll retaliate?"

"Probably will, in some way or another."

"So we just wait until they do?"

"Well, they ain't breaking the law, are they?" I looked at Ross.

"No, I reckon not."

"So we wait until they do," I said.

"But shouldn't we do something to prepare ourselves?" Ross protested.

"Like what?"

"We could make up some new laws to make it easier for us to keep the peace," Ross suggested.

"What sorta laws?" I asked, curious.

"Well, we could make it illegal to carry a gun in town."

I didn't reply as I thought on that.

"It would make it easier to keep the peace," Ross added.

"I'll think on it," I said, and Ross nodded.

Chapter eighteen

Things were quiet that afternoon, so that evening I rode out to the Tomlin's ranch and ate supper with them. Desperate seemed glad to get out of a stall, and we trotted briskly.

We ate supper, and then everyone went out onto the porch.

"Seems like old times," I smiled as I sat next to Rachel.

"I miss this," Rachel pouted.

"Me too," I said softly.

"Well, how's the new job?" Mr. Tomlin spoke up.

"We've been busy," I replied, and I told them all that had happened.

Rachel looked disturbed when I told them about Scar-face, and then she looked worried when I told them about Virgil.

Afterwards, it was silent as everyone took in everything, and then Mr. Tomlin cleared his throat.

"You watch Ike Nash," he warned. "He's no good."

"I will," I replied. "In fact, Ross and I are thinking on ways to keep the peace."

"Oh? Like what?"

"Ross suggested passing a law that makes it illegal to carry a gun in town," I explained.

As soon as I said that, Mr. Tomlin scowled and looked displeased.

"If you think I'm going to hand over my gun every time I come to town, you are mistaken," he said in a stern voice.

"What?" I asked, startled.

"To disarm everybody is the last thing you want," Mr. Tomlin continued. "All the honest folks will obey, and then all it would take is for one of Ike's gunmen to come to town while you and Ross are gone, and he could wipe the entire town out."

"I hadn't thought of that," I admitted.

49

"Instead of disarming folks, you should arm everybody that can hold a gun," Mr. Tomlin said. "Ike's hands would behave themselves if they knew everybody in town was armed and willing to shoot back."

I nodded soberly as I thought on that.

"Yes, I believe you're right," I said.

"Course I am."

"We won't be disarming folks then," I said with a sheepish grin.

"I'm glad to hear that," Mr. Tomlin nodded emphatically.

After that we talked a bit more, and then it was time for me to go. I thanked Mrs. Tomlin for supper, and Rachel walked with me to my horse.

"How are you holding up?" Rachel asked, and added, "After killing Scar-face?"

"Tell you the truth, I haven't had much time to think about it," I said.

Rachel nodded and asked, "How's the house?"

"It's fine, just fine," I grinned.

"I'd like to see it sometime," she hinted.

"I'd like for you to see it too," I said, and then my face turned dark. "Soon as the boarders are gone, that is."

"Boarders?"

I told her about Lee, Brian, and Ross.

"I thought this house was for us," Rachel objected.

"It is," I said, and added, "Don't worry. They won't be staying long."

"They'd better not," she said. It was silent, and she asked, "What's going to happen with Virgil?"

"Not sure," I admitted.

"I don't like this."

"Me neither," I smiled.

"Do you think he could-," Rachel paused and frowned.

"Kill me?" I finished her sentence.

Rachel bit her lower lip and nodded.

I frowned as I thought on that. I turned it around in my head, studied it from all angles, and decided.

"No," I declared. "I don't."

"How can you be so sure?" Rachel looked at me with big eyes.

"I just know," I said.

Chapter nineteen

The next day was Sunday. The Tomlins came to town for church, and I went with them.

I spent some time with Rachel that afternoon. We walked around town, and I showed her the outside of the house. I wanted to show her the inside, but my three boarders were busy taking a nap.

I could tell Rachel wanted a glimpse of Virgil. But he never showed, and I was glad.

The building crew for the hotel arrived midafternoon. I woke Lee and Brian, and they hustled about as they got everyone settled.

Evening time arrived all too quickly. I took Rachel home, and when I got back Ross and I took a stroll around town. All was quiet, so we turned in early.

Monday morning found Ross and me sitting on the porch at the jail, drinking coffee and playing chess as usual.

The building crew was hard at work, and we had a good view from the porch. Lee and Brian were supervising, and I was amused as I watched Lee hustle about.

"I don't think I've ever seen Lee work this hard," I commented as I took a swig of coffee.

"He does seem to be motivated," Ross observed.

"Does," I agreed, and added, "I think I know who's motivating him."

"Who?"

"A woman."

Ross smiled.

"Funny, the things a man will do for a woman," he said.

I looked down at my badge and nodded.

"Sure is," I said.

***

The morning passed quickly. Ross and I played several games of chess, and Ross won easily. However, with each game my understanding of the game improved.

We were still playing chess when the stagecoach arrived.

I was mulling over the chessboard, and Ross was watching me with a wry smile. I frowned hesitantly and moved, and Ross's smile widened as he took my bishop.

I sighed in disgust and glanced at the stage.

There was only one passenger. It was a woman, and she carried a small carpetbag. She looked up and down the street, and then she walked toward us.

She was a little travel-worn, but she was still good looking with long blond hair.

She wore a red dress with a low neck that looked expensive. She also wore make-up, and I guessed her to be in her early twenties.

Ross looked up from our game and spotted her, and we both watched as she passed by. She noticed us, and she smiled and gave a small curtsy.

We smiled back. Her eyes lingered on us, and then she went inside the hotel.

I glanced at Ross, and he was frowning at me.

"What were you looking at?" He challenged.

"I reckon the same thing you were looking at," I grinned.

"I should tell Rachel."

"Tell her what?" I asked defensively. "Besides, you looked too."

"But I don't have Rachel," Ross said, and then he reminded, "But you do. That means you ain't allowed to look."

"I declare," I gasped. "She walked right in front of us. Am I supposed to look the other way?"

"Yes," Ross declared, and then asked, "Who do you suppose she is?"

53

"Seeing how I can't even look at her, how am I supposed to find that out?" I asked, perplexed.

Ross ignored me as he stood.

"Think I'll go introduce myself," he said.

"Want me to come along?" I offered.

"I do not."

"What about our game?" I beckoned at the chessboard.

"We'll finish it later," Ross replied, and then he was gone.

Chapter twenty

I chuckled as I watched Ross disappear into the hotel. I filled my cup with fresh coffee and leaned back.

A few minutes passed, and I spotted Butch Nelson riding into town. He nodded as he passed by.

"Sheriff," he said.

"Butch," I nodded back.

"Pleasant day."

"So far," I agreed with a tight smile.

He rode on down to the hotel and dismounted. He tied his horse to the hitching rail and walked inside.

I couldn't help but be curious, and I frowned thoughtfully.

I was still sitting there, deep in thought, when Ross returned.

"Her name is Lucy Wells," he announced.

"Who?"

"The lady from the stage."

"Oh. Her. I had forgotten," I said.

"Sure you did," Ross drawled as he sat next to me.

"What happened?" I asked.

"Nothing much. When I got there she was getting a room. I introduced myself and told her if there was anything she needed to let me know."

"Did she say what she's doing here?"

"No, she didn't talk much. She seemed tired."

I nodded, and it fell silent as we sat there. A few minutes passed, and I spotted some movement down the street.

It was Lucy, coming out of the hotel.

"Thought you said she was tired," I gestured.

Ross looked up, and we watched as she hustled down the street. She passed us, and we smiled again. She smiled back and gave another small curtsy.

She stopped at the livery stable.

There was an older boy named Mike cleaning out horse stalls, and she talked to him. Next, she gave him a folded piece of paper and some money, and then she turned and headed back toward us while Mike disappeared inside.

Lucy glanced at us as she drew close, and Ross grinned and stood.

"Hello again, Miss Wells," he said.

"Please, call me Lucy," she beamed as she stopped in front of us. She smiled at Ross, and then she looked at me. "Who is this?"

"I'm Rondo Landon, ma'am," I said.

"You're Rondo Landon?" She exclaimed, and her eyes grew wide.

"That's me."

"What a thrill it is to meet you!" She squealed.

"Same here," I smiled pleasantly.

Ross shot me a dark look and stepped in front of me.

"Yeah, me and ol' Rondo here are good friends," he drawled, and added helpfully, "In fact, I'll probably be in his wedding. He's getting married soon."

"Oh?" Lucy looked disappointed.

"Mebbe I could show you the town sometime?" Ross offered.

"That would be nice," Lucy tried to look pleasant.

While they talked, I noticed Mike from the livery stable. He was a-horseback, and he trotted briskly down the street and left town.

I frowned in thought, and then I heard my name being mentioned. I looked up and noticed that Lucy and Ross were looking at me.

"I'm sorry. What did you say?" I asked.

"I was just telling Lucy about you and Rachel," Ross said. "I was thinking we could all go on a picnic sometime."

"Oh. Sure," I smiled.

Ross grinned and looked at Lucy.

56

"It's settled then?" He asked.

"Let me think on it," Lucy said politely.

"Sure, take all the time you need," Ross said, and he tried to hide his disappointment.

"We'll talk again," Lucy promised, and then she looked at me. "Goodbye now."

I nodded, and we watched as she walked down the street.

"She's a real nice lady, ain't she?" Ross said wistfully.

"I reckon so," I nodded.

Butch Nelson stepped out right as Lucy approached the hotel. He held the door open for her, and then he walked over to his horse and mounted up.

I was curious as Butch kicked up his horse.

"I'll be back," I told Ross.

Ross nodded, and I walked toward the hotel.

Chapter twenty-one

Butch spotted Rondo sitting on the porch at the jail as he rode into town.

They exchanged a few words, and then Butch went on to the hotel. He dismounted, tied his horse to the hitching rail, and walked inside.

Virgil Carson sat in the parlor, eating a biscuit and drinking coffee. Butch spotted him and walked over.

"Butch," Virgil said.

"Virgil," Butch nodded. "Mind if I sit?"

"Go ahead," Virgil said. "Have some coffee."

Butch sat and poured a cup, and it was silent as he blew softly into the cup.

"Something on your mind?" Virgil asked.

"Ike Nash wanted me to come see you."

"What about?"

"Ike wants me to be the next sheriff," Butch announced.

"Congratulations," Virgil's face was emotionless.

"And, to make me look better to the town folks, he wants me to run you out of town soon as you kill Rondo," Butch informed.

Virgil looked up and stared at Butch.

"That's why I'm here," Butch explained. "Ike is willing to pay. There'll be no need for trouble."

"No," Virgil said quietly.

"Why not?" Butch was surprised.

"Nobody tells me what to do."

"I ain't telling you what to do," Butch argued. "Ike wants to hire you to leave town. Everything would be real peaceful."

"I already told you my answer," Virgil said bluntly.

Butch narrowed his eyes.

"Agreement or not, I'll still run you out of town," he warned.

58

"Think you're good enough?"

"Yes."

"Well then. You do what you have to do, and I'll do the same," Virgil said.

Butch finished his coffee in one gulp and stood.

"I reckon we understand one another," he said.

"We do," Virgil agreed.

Butch scowled and walked out of the hotel.

Chapter twenty-two

After Butch was gone, I walked into the hotel and looked around.

Sitting in the parlor was Virgil Carson. He had just finished breakfast, and was drinking coffee.

I breathed deeply and walked over to him. He glanced up, and several seconds passed as we looked at each other.

"Virgil," I said. "Mind if I sit?"

"Go ahead," he said.

I eased into a chair. Meanwhile, Virgil took another swig of coffee and wiped his mouth with a napkin.

"You're the second visitor I've had this morning," Virgil said. "Butch Nelson was just in to see me too."

"I saw him."

"You've got a lot of enemies."

"Oh?" I asked, curious.

Virgil didn't explain. Instead, he asked, "What do you want?"

"Understanding," I said.

"Don't we all," Virgil said, and asked, "Understanding about what?"

"You remind me of someone."

"Who?"

"Ben Kinrich," I announced.

A hint of surprise showed in Virgil's eyes. He nodded, and it was silent while he studied me.

"I reckon now is as good a time as any," he finally said, and asked, "Did he ever mention me?"

"Who?" I asked.

"Ben Kinrich."

"You knew Ben?"

Virgil didn't reply. He took a swig of coffee, looked around the room, and glanced back at me.

"You never wondered how Ben did it?"

"Did what?" I asked, confused.

"Planned the jobs."

"Can't say I did," I admitted.

Virgil scowled, as if he was disappointed with me.

"How long was Ben gone when he left to plan the jobs?" Virgil asked.

"Most times, only two, three days," I recalled.

"And how far away were the jobs?" Virgil pressed.

"Sometimes, it took us weeks to get there," I said, and I frowned in confusion as I thought on that.

"Every job Ben pulled was always planned extremely well," Virgil continued. "When ya'll were in your canyon, did you ever see him planning things out?"

"No."

"So how did he do it?" Virgil asked, and there was sarcasm in his voice.

I shook my head in amazement as understanding began to dawn on me.

"He had a partner," I said softly.

"That's right," Virgil nodded. "Me."

"He never told me."

"Ben sure told me a lot about you," Virgil scowled. "Said he was teaching you how to use a Colt, and he also told me about your plans for the cattle business. He wanted the three of us to go in together."

"How did you know Ben?" I asked.

"I raised him."

"Ben's folks were killed by Comanches when he was a boy," I recalled.

"That's right," Virgil nodded. "I came by on a cattle drive a few days later and picked him up. From then on he lived with me. When he got older we pulled a few jobs together, but then I caught a bullet in the lung. That's when he organized his own outfit. Once I recovered, we decided I would stay on the outside and plan the jobs."

"Why didn't he tell me?" I asked, perplexed.

61

"That was our agreement," Virgil said. "Nobody was to know about me. That gave me the freedom to scout and plan all the jobs. Things were working fine until you showed up. I was against you joining up, but Ben had the same feelings for you that I had for him. But then you killed him."

It fell silent as I thought on everything. It was a lot to take in, and I took my time.

"And now you want to kill me," I finally said.

"That is correct."

I started to reply, but Virgil cut me off.

"And there's nothing you can do or say that will change my mind," Virgil declared. "Ben was like a son to me."

"But he had to be stopped," I protested. "He went crazy; you can't deny that."

"He didn't snap until you betrayed him," Virgil declared, and anger showed in his eyes. "You quit on him when he needed you the most."

"I quit because it was the right thing to do," I argued.

Virgil snorted in disgust and looked away.

"I won't fight you," I declared. "Not over this."

Surprise showed in Virgil's face, and he looked back at me.

"You won't face me?"

"That is correct," I said, and added, "I want you to leave town."

"I'm not going anywhere," Virgil declared, "until the business between us is settled."

"I'll run you out," I warned.

"Go ahead and try," Virgil scoffed.

I frowned at that, and then I stood.

"We'll talk about this some more," I said.

"I'll be here," Virgil said.

I didn't reply as I walked out the door.

Chapter twenty-three

Later that afternoon, Ross and I sat on the porch at the jail. We drank coffee and played chess, and I also told Ross about my conversation with Virgil.

"What are you going to do?" Ross asked.

"Not sure yet."

"You could run him outta town," Ross suggested.

"He invited me to try," I said wryly.

"We could both go," Ross reasoned. "He might be more reasonable with a shotgun in his face."

I smiled at that.

"Even if we did, he would just come back," I replied. "He's the sort that doesn't give up."

Ross frowned thoughtfully, and it fell silent as we played our game. I moved, and Ross smiled as he took my queen.

"This is an irritating game," I complained.

"If you allow it, chess can teach you a lot," Ross replied.

"How so?"

"A well-played game of chess has a logical crispness about it," Ross lectured. "It can teach you memory, patience, and tactical maneuvers."

"Chess teaches you all that?"

"Sure it does."

I frowned as I moved again, and then I leaned back in my chair. I nodded at some folks as they passed by, and they nodded back.

"Since I've been sheriff, seems like all we do is sit here playing chess and drinking coffee," I said. "Seems like we should be doing something."

"We are," Ross replied as he moved. "We're keeping the peace."

I frowned at that, and then a thought suddenly occurred to me.

"I know something we can do," I announced.

"What's that?" Ross looked at me.

"I talked to Fred's wife yesterday at church," I explained. "She's the schoolteacher."

Ross nodded.

"She's been giving Jeremiah Batch private reading and writing lessons once a week, but he hasn't showed up in two weeks," I said. "In fact, nobody's seen him."

"Think something happened to him?"

"I hope not," I replied. "But, I think we should ride out and check on him."

"Now?"

"Too late today," I replied. "We'll ride out in the morning."

Ross nodded, and I frowned as I studied the chessboard.

"Whose turn is it?" I asked.

Ross looked thoughtful.

"Can't remember," he admitted.

"I thought chess was supposed to give you a sharp memory," I retorted.

Ross looked sharply at me, and we both chuckled.

Chapter twenty-four

That evening Ross and I took a stroll around town again.

All was quiet, so I walked back up the street to where Lee and Brian's hotel was being built. The crew had quit for the day, but Lee and Brian were still there, planning things for the next day.

"What do you think?" Lee asked.

"Looks like a lot of wood lying about," I commented as I looked around.

"We'll have the walls up by the end of the week," Lee declared.

I nodded, and then I squinted as I looked down the street.

Mike the livery boy was trotting back into town. He pulled up in front of the livery stable, and he dismounted and started unsaddling his horse.

"Join us for supper?" Lee asked.

"Sure," I said. "I'll meet you at the café."

Lee nodded, and I walked down the street towards the livery stable.

"Evening, Sheriff," Mike said as I walked up.

"Mike," I nodded. "Busy day?"

"Yes, sir," he nodded.

I followed him inside as he led his horse into a stall.

"Did you deliver a message for Miss Wells?" I asked.

"Who?"

"The lady from the stage."

"Oh. Yes, I did," Mike said, and added, "I had to ride all the way out to Ike Nash's headquarters."

I was startled.

"You delivered a message to Ike?"

"No, it was for his son, Tanner."

I pinched my face in thought.

"I don't suppose you read it?"

65

"I did not," Mike looked startled. "That wouldn't have been right."

"It wouldn't have," I agreed, and then I turned to leave. "Well, have a good evening."

"You too, Sheriff."

I nodded and headed towards the café.

Chapter twenty-five

The café was crowded.

Lee and Brian had a table in the back. I made my way over to them and sat.

Everybody's attention was occupied. I turned and looked, and I spotted Lucy Wells. She was seated at the piano in the corner, playing a song I'd never heard before.

She had freshened up and changed clothes. The dress she wore now was blue, and it was even fancier than the one she'd had on earlier.

Ross was sitting at the closest table next to her, and he was listening intently to every note.

She wasn't very good, but nobody seemed to notice. She played loud and was pretty, and that seemed to be good enough.

"Where did she come from?" Brian asked.

"Came on the stage today," I explained.

"I can't tell if that piano is out of tune, or if she's hitting the wrong notes," Brian said.

"Probably a little of both," I suggested.

A waiter brought us some coffee and took our order. While we waited, Lee frowned as he studied her.

"Who is she?" Lee asked.

"Her name is Lucy Wells," I said.

"Know anything about her?"

"Not much," I shook my head. "All I know is that she sent Ike Nash's son a message today."

Lee frowned thoughtfully, but he didn't say anything. The waiter brought our food, and it was silent as we ate.

Afterwards, Brian and I drank some more coffee while Lee pulled out a cigar. He bit off the end, struck a match on the table, and lit his cigar.

"I can't be sure, but it seems like I've seen her before," Lee declared as he took a puff.

"Oh?" I prompted.

"It was back when I was meeting the Oltman brothers up at Abilene," Lee explained. "You remember them?"

"Uh-huh," I frowned.

"We met in a saloon and had a few drinks before we left out," Lee continued. "There was a girl there that looked a lot like her."

"A saloon girl?"

"She was more than that."

"Oh," I said, and it was silent as we thought on that.

"Mebbe she came here for a fresh start," Brian suggested.

"Mebbe so," Lee said, and added, "She was broke in Abilene, but now she dresses like a queen. I wonder how she can afford it?"

"Somebody must have given her money," I surmised.

"Well, I could be wrong," Lee said. "But, it sure looks like her."

"I don't reckon it really matters," I replied. "As long as she doesn't break the law, she's no concern of mine."

"I'd be concerned," Lee disagreed.

"About what?" I asked.

"Your deputy."

We all looked at Ross. He had a lopsided grin on his face, and he was tapping his foot to the music.

"He does seem to be smitten," Brian observed.

"Looks like," I agreed, and added, "Whoever she is, I'm not going to judge her past. Anyone can change. The three of us are examples of that."

"I haven't changed," Lee objected.

I scowled at Lee, but didn't reply.

Chapter twenty-six

We were in no hurry to leave. Lee smoked another cigar while Brian and I drank another pot of coffee.

Lucy finally ran out of songs to play. Most everybody in the room applauded as she stood and gave a small curtsy.

Ross clapped the loudest and the longest.

"That was wonderful!" We heard him say. "Your playing reminds me of my mama. She played a lot when I was a youngster."

"Oh, that's sweet," Lucy smiled politely, and asked, "I am very tired. Would you escort me to my room?"

"I'd be glad too!" Ross beamed.

He took Lucy's hand, and he grinned from ear to ear as they walked toward the door.

"Yep," Brian drawled after they were gone, "Your deputy is hooked."

"I'd say so," I agreed.

"I wonder if Ross's mama wore fancy dresses like that?" Lee chuckled.

"I doubt it," I replied as I stood. "Well, think I'll take a stroll around town. See you later."

They nodded, and I left. I walked down all the main streets, and all was quiet.

I was approaching the hotel when I spotted a rider coming into town. I backed into the shadows and stood still as I studied him.

He was young, and I could tell that he had a cocky way about him. In fact, the way he acted reminded me some of Ryan Palmer. He was tall, slim, and wore a Colt on his hip.

He dismounted in front of the hotel, tied his horse to the railing, and walked inside.

I couldn't help but be curious. I waited a few seconds, and then I followed him into the lobby.

I was just in time to see him go up the stairs. He reached the top and disappeared down the hallway.

"Evening, Sheriff," the hotel clerk said.

"Evening," I nodded back.

"Help you?"

"Did you see the young fella that just came in?" I asked.

"Yes," he nodded.

"Recognize him?"

"Of course," the hotel clerk said. "That was Tanner Nash."

"Did you talk to him?" I asked.

"Sure. He wanted to know Lucy Well's room number."

I frowned at that and nodded.

"'Preciate it," I said.

"Anytime, Sheriff."

Chapter twenty-seven

Ross talked nonstop while they walked toward the hotel. Lucy pretended to be interested, and she managed to smile every once in a while.

They reached the hotel. Ross escorted her to her room, and Lucy promptly said goodnight.

"I'll see you tomorrow," Ross said.

"Yes," Lucy forced a smile. "Goodbye now."

"Yes, ma'am," Ross grinned back, and then he was gone.

Lucy rolled her eyes and shut the door. She poured some water and washed her face, and then she heard a knock.

She frowned irritably.

"Yes, what do you want?" She asked as she opened the door.

Tanner Nash stood in the doorway, and she uttered a small cry of surprise.

Tanner's eyes lit up, and they rushed into each other's arms. They embraced and kissed.

"You got my message," Lucy said.

"I did," Tanner said, and then he frowned. He released her and walked over to the window. "You shouldn't have done that, Lucy. What if my father had seen it? Besides, we agreed not to meet for another month."

"I couldn't wait any longer. I just had to see you," Lucy replied, and then she frowned. "After all, I am your wife."

"Did you tell anyone that?" A concerned look crossed Tanner's face.

"Of course not. You told me not to," Lucy replied. "And believe me, I wanted to. The deputy here is quite taken with me."

"Did he cause you trouble?" Tanner's face darkened.

71

"No, I can handle him," Lucy reassured. "That's why I'm keeping his hopes up. Other folks will leave me alone if they think I'm interested in him."

"Good," Tanner looked relieved.

"But I'd rather be known as your wife," Lucy declared. "Why do we have to hide?"

"My father," Tanner explained. "He's going to explode when he finds out."

"You've already had three weeks," Lucy protested. "Why haven't you told him?"

"We've had trouble," Tanner said, and he explained about killing Jeremiah Batch.

Lucy listened, and she looked displeased as she thought on it.

"So, when are you going to tell him about us?"

"As soon as things settle down," Tanner promised.

"And how long will that be?"

"Two, three weeks at the most."

"I have to stay here that long?" Lucy protested.

"I'll visit every chance I have."

Lucy didn't reply. She joined Tanner at the window, and her face was thoughtful.

"Three weeks," she said.

"Three weeks," Tanner repeated, and added, "I promise."

"I guess I can wait that long," Lucy said, and Tanner grinned.

Chapter twenty-eight

We turned in early, and I cooked breakfast again for my three boarders the next morning.

After breakfast, Ross and I saddled our horses and rode out.

It was a five-mile ride to Jeremiah's headquarters. Our horses were fresh, so we trotted along briskly.

It was open, rolling land, covered in grass. The grass was green, and Desperate occasionally nipped at it.

"Jeremiah has a lot of grass this year," I commented.

"His cows should be fat," Ross agreed.

"There's some over there," I pointed to a faraway hill.

They were a long ways off, and Ross squinted as he studied them.

"Jeremiah must have grown his herd some," Ross noted.

"Looks like it," I agreed, and added, "Well, least he has the grass for it."

Ross nodded, and it fell silent as we trotted along.

"So, what do you think?" Ross finally broke the silence.

"About what?"

"Lucy."

"Oh. Her," I frowned. I hesitated, and said, "She seems nice enough."

"I think she likes me," Ross beamed.

I didn't reply. Instead, I just nodded.

***

Jeremiah was old and couldn't afford any help. Because of that, the ranch headquarters was in bad shape. The pole corrals sagged and the barn was about to fall down.

However, as we rode up we noticed that the corrals had been repaired, and the barn had been rebuilt. There were also several horses in the corrals.

73

"Jeremiah's been busy," Ross noted.

"Somebody has," I replied.

We heard the sound of hammering. We looked over at the house, and there were two young fellers working on the roof.

"Looks like Jeremiah hired some help," Ross commented.

I pinched my face in thought as we rode over.

I didn't know how, but for some reason I knew that Jeremiah was dead.

Something snapped inside of me as soon as I realized that, and I felt an odd feeling deep inside. It was sorta like what I'd felt before, only more hostile and irritable.

They spotted us and climbed down. Their rifles were on the porch, and they stood by them.

One was bigger than the other.

The bigger one stood over six feet tall, and he had a muscled torso with dark hair. The smaller one was leaner and had red hair.

I recognized the bigger one. He had been in town the night I killed Scar-face.

"What do you want?" The bigger one demanded.

I ignored his question as I dismounted. Ross did the same, and we walked up to them and stopped.

"Morning," I said.

"What do you want?" He asked again.

"I have a few questions," I said.

"I ain't gonna tell you anything," he sneered, and then he stuck his face within inches of mine. "You killed a friend of mine the other night. You'd best git before I get ugly."

Without saying a word, I palmed my Colt with a fast but easy movement. I struck him in the side of the face, and he fell backwards. I holstered my Colt as he hit the ground.

74

My face was emotionless while he grimaced in pain and rolled around on the ground. Meanwhile, Ross and the smaller one jumped in surprise.

"You cracked my skull!" He screamed.

"I bet it hurts too," I said, and asked, "You gonna answer my questions now?"

He sat up and glared at me. Blood ran from his nose and dribbled off his chin.

"What do you wanna know?" He asked in a subdued voice.

"Who do you ride for?"

"Ike Nash," he said.

"What's your name?"

"Brock Jackson."

I nodded and looked at the smaller one.

"And you?"

He swallowed nervously and said, "I'm Rory. Rory Wheeler."

"Where is Jeremiah?" I asked them.

"Who?" Brock asked.

"He owns the ranch," I explained.

"No, he doesn't," Brock snorted.

Soon as he said that, Rory looked down at the ground.

"Then who does?" I narrowed my eyes.

"Ike Nash," Brock said.

I glanced at Ross and looked back at Brock.

"What happened to Jeremiah?" I asked.

"Who says anything happened to him?"

I frowned at that. It fell silent, and Rory shifted his feet nervously.

"How 'bout you?" I asked Rory. "You know anything?"

Brock gave him a threatening glare, and Rory swallowed hard and shook his head.

"No, sir," he said quietly.

"We don't know nothing," Brock spoke back up. "You want to know anything else, mebbe you should talk to Ike."

"That ain't a bad idea," I agreed. "Think we'll ride over there."

Brock grunted, and it fell silent again.

Brock glared at me, and I met his glare for several seconds. Then, I looked at Rory.

He tried to meet my look, but couldn't. He swallowed hard and looked away.

"Jeremiah Batch was a good man," I told them. "I won't quit looking until I find out what happened to him."

Neither one replied as we turned and mounted up.

We trotted briskly until we were out of gunshot range, and then we slowed our pace.

Ross shot me an irritated look.

"Brock wasn't doing anything wrong, Rondo," Ross said. "As Sheriff, you shouldn't have hit him."

"He was bothersome," I replied.

"But what you did was illegal," Ross objected.

"No," I disagreed. "It was personal."

Chapter twenty-nine

"That ranch was all Jeremiah had," I told Ross while we trotted towards Ike Nash's headquarters. "He wouldn't sell, unless he was forced."

"Think Ike forced him?"

"I'm afraid he did more than that."

Ross nodded, and it fell silent. It was a short ride, and an hour later we rode up on a hill that overlooked headquarters.

Ike's headquarters was in a meadow, with a stream. The pole corrals were well built and in good shape. There was a bunkhouse, and the main house was long and big.

"Nice layout," I commented.

"Ike has a lot of money," Ross explained.

"It shows," I said, and then I kicked up Desperate.

We rode up in front of the main house and pulled up. Several ranch hands spotted us from the bunkhouse, and they gathered around us.

I recognized a few of them from town, and they didn't look very happy to see us. In fact, a few of them even looked hateful.

I glanced at Ross, and he looked worried.

It was silent, and then Butch Nelson stepped out onto the porch. He seemed surprised to see us.

"What are you doing here, Sheriff?" He asked.

"We came to see Ike."

A look of amusement crossed Butch's face.

"I'll take you to him," he said.

I nodded. We dismounted, tied our horses to the hitching rail, and followed Butch inside.

"Wait here," Butch told us in the parlor, and then he disappeared down the hallway.

The parlor was elegant. Everything was made out of wood, and there was a fancy chandelier hanging from the ceiling.

Butch reappeared a few minutes later.

"He'll see you now," he said.

"Figured he would," I said, and we followed Butch to the study.

It was an impressive room. There was the smell of cigar smoke, and there was also a fireplace. There was a big desk in the corner, and Ike Nash sat behind it.

"So you're Rondo Landon," Ike said with a deep, booming voice. "I've heard a lot about you."

"I've heard of you too," I replied.

"Sit," he offered, so we did. Meanwhile, Butch sat behind us.

"Want anything to drink?" Ike offered.

"No thanks," I said, and added, "We came here to find out what happened to Jeremiah Batch."

Ike chuckled.

"I've heard you're direct," he said.

"I am," I nodded, and continued, "We talked to Brock and Rory. They said you own Jeremiah's ranch."

"That's right."

"You bought it?"

"Yes, two weeks ago."

It was silent as I thought on that, and then I cleared my throat.

"Do you have any proof?"

"Of course," he nodded and looked at Butch. "Butch, fetch the bill of sale from my safe."

Butch stood. He walked over to a safe in the corner, opened it, and pulled out a stack of papers. He sorted through them, pulled one out, and handed it to Ike.

Ike looked at it and nodded.

"Here it is," he handed it to me.

I looked it over, and I frowned when I noticed Jeremiah's signature.

"Is this Jeremiah's mark?"

"That's right," Ike said. "He couldn't write."

"That's odd," I glanced at Ross. "Jeremiah's been taking reading and writing lessons for months now. Last I heard, he was writing good."

Ike didn't reply, and his face remained blank.

"Interesting, ain't it?" I asked Ike.

"Maybe he was nervous," Ike suggested, and there was a warning in his voice.

"So what happened to Jeremiah?" I asked as I handed the bill of sale back to Ike. "Nobody's seen him."

"He told me he had some family back east," Ike said. "I reckon he went there."

"I wonder why he didn't tell anybody goodbye?" I asked.

"He must have been in a hurry," Ike suggested, and asked, "Is there anything else? I have a busy day."

"No, I found out what I came for," I replied. Ross and I stood, and then I added, "I'm going to find out what happened to Jeremiah."

"I just told you what happened," Ike looked displeased.

I didn't reply. Instead, I asked, "Did Butch give you the list?"

"Oh, yes. I had forgotten," Ike said. He pulled out his wallet, grabbed a few big bills, and gave them to me. "Here. This should cover everything."

"I'll get you some change," I said as I folded the bills and put them in my pocket.

"No need," he waved his hand at me.

Ross and I walked to the door, but then I stopped.

"I hear you've been buying ranches all over Texas," I said.

"That's right," Ike nodded.

"What exactly are you after?" I narrowed my eyes.

79

"I want it all," Ike declared.

"All of what?"

"All I can get," Ike said softly.

I didn't reply. It was silent as we looked at each other, and then we left.

Chapter thirty

"What do we do now?" Ross asked as we trotted back to town.

"We figure out what happened to Jeremiah," I replied.

"How do we do that?"

"I was hoping you'd have a suggestion."

Ross frowned in thought, and then he replied, "You want to know how I beat you at chess?"

"Because you're better than I am?"

"That's partly the reason," Ross smiled. "But mostly, what I do is set up my defense, and then wait for you to mess up."

I frowned and grunted.

"Our little visit will probably stir things up," Ross continued. "I say we sit back and see what develops. Let them make a mistake."

I thought on that and nodded.

"Not much else we can do," I reasoned.

Ross nodded, and asked, "When did Fred's wife tell you Jeremiah could write?"

"She didn't," I replied, and added, "But Ike doesn't know that."

Ross frowned at that, and it fell silent as we trotted on to town.

***

As soon as we got back, we unsaddled and tended to our horses. It was suppertime, so we ate at the café and then took a stroll around town.

All was quiet.

Afterwards, Ross hurried back to the café, hoping to see Lucy, and I went to the sheriff's office.

81

I made some coffee. Lee and Brian showed up, and we sat out on the porch. Brian and I drank coffee while Lee smoked a cigar.

"I see you're getting the walls up," I noted as I looked down the street.

"We've made good progress," Lee nodded, and then he asked, "Where have you and Ross been today?"

I told them about Jeremiah, and they frowned as they thought on it.

"You think he's dead," Lee surmised.

"I know Jeremiah. He wouldn't have left without saying something," I replied.

"You think Ike killed him?"

"I think he's responsible."

Lee sighed as he took a puff on his cigar.

"I'm starting to think it would have been more peaceful if we had built our hotel in another town," he complained.

"But not near as interesting," I pointed out.

Lee smiled, and it fell silent as we drank our coffee.

A few minutes later, I spotted someone riding into town.

He rode by us and dismounted in front of the hotel. He tied his horse to the hitching rail and went inside.

"Who was that?" Lee asked.

"Tanner Nash," I replied.

Lee looked thoughtful.

"Interesting," he said.

"Yes," I agreed. "It is."

Chapter thirty-one

Virgil came to see me the next morning.

We had just finished breakfast, and we were sitting on the porch at the jail, drinking our morning coffee. Lee and Brian were also there.

"Virgil," I said as he walked up.

"Rondo," he replied.

"Coffee?"

Virgil hesitated, but then nodded. I poured him some, and it was silent while we drank our coffee.

"It's time," Virgil finally said.

"For what?" I asked.

"To do what I came here to do."

I frowned at that.

"I already said I wouldn't face you," I said.

"You'll change your mind when I start shooting," Virgil responded, and added, "I'll be in the street this evening at six o'clock."

"Well, I won't," I declared.

Frustration showed in Virgil's face.

"If you don't show, I'll come for you," he threatened.

Before I could respond, Lee cleared his throat.

"Rondo might not be in the street at six, but I will," he said softly.

We all shot Lee a startled look.

"This ain't your fight," Virgil objected.

"I'm making it my fight."

"I'll be there too," Ross suddenly blurted.

Everyone gave Ross a startled look, and then we all looked at Brian. He frowned, and then sighed.

"Why not," he said. "I'll be there too."

Virgil's face turned red with anger as he glared at us.

"My fight's not with you three; it's with Rondo," he declared, and then he looked at me. "One way or the other,

83

you're going to face me. You can't hide behind your friends forever."

I didn't reply. It was silent, and Virgil turned and left.

We watched as he went back to the hotel, and then I cleared my throat.

"I don't know what to say," I said, deeply humbled.

"Then don't say anything," Lee said, and he glanced at Brian. "You ready?"

"Let's go," Brian nodded.

"See you later," Lee told us, and they headed towards their hotel.

I was speechless as I watched them go, and then I turned to Ross.

"Thanks, Ross," I said earnestly.

"Tell you the truth, I only said it because Lee said it first," Ross admitted with a sheepish grin. "I'd be terrified if I had to face Virgil alone."

"Most folks would be," I replied.

"But you wouldn't."

"No, I reckon not," I said truthfully.

Ross pinched his face in thought.

"You reckon you can be brave and scared at the same time?" He asked.

It was silent as I pondered that.

"I think when you're scared is the only time you *can* be brave," I finally replied.

Ross nodded slowly.

"You might be right," he said.

Chapter thirty-two

That afternoon I gave the town council the money from Ike.

They were pleased. There was more than enough to pay for all the damages, including the doctor bill for Morgan's son.

"How is your son?" I asked Morgan.

"Recovery is slow, but we're getting there," he replied.

"Good," I said.

***

That evening, Ross and I took a stroll around town. Afterwards, we stopped at the café and ate supper.

"Lucy got a part-time job, playing the piano," Ross announced as we found a table. "The owner hopes it'll attract more customers."

"I'm sure her playing will attract some attention," I said wryly.

Ross didn't reply, and I wasn't sure if he had even heard me.

Lucy was playing the piano, and Ross gave her his full attention. Like before, her playing was loud and off-key, but Ross didn't seem to notice.

We ate, and afterwards Lucy took a break. She came over and sat with us.

"Sounds wonderful," Ross beamed.

"Thank you, kind sir," Lucy said coyly.

"How long have you played the piano?" I spoke up.

"Since I was little," Lucy replied. "But, until yesterday, I haven't played in a long time."

"I can tell," I said.

A puzzled look crossed Lucy's face, and I could tell she wasn't sure how to take my remark.

After that, Lucy and Ross made pleasant conversation while I just sat there and drank coffee.

I drank four cups, and then Rory Wheeler walked in. He wore a Colt and looked nervous.

I shifted in my chair so that my gun hand was free.

"You see him?" I asked Ross in a quiet voice.

"See who?" Lucy asked, confused.

"It's Rory," Ross said.

"He's armed," I warned.

Ross nodded, and Lucy's eyes grew wide with excitement as she watched us.

Rory stood by the door while his eyes adjusted, and then he looked around the room. He spotted us and walked over.

"Sheriff," he said in a small, timid voice. "I was looking for you."

"You found me," I said, and then I nodded at Lucy. "This is Miss Lucy Wells. You already know Ross."

"Ma'am," Rory nodded.

Lucy nodded back. She was attentive, and she seemed to be interested.

"I came here to confess," Rory suddenly blurted.

"Confess to what?" Ross spoke up.

"I know who killed Jeremiah," he said, and his lip trembled.

We were all startled, and then I frowned.

"So Jeremiah is dead?"

"He's dead," Rory nodded sullenly.

Before he could say more, I turned to Lucy.

"Could you excuse us, Lucy? We need to talk to this fella alone."

It was obvious that Lucy didn't want to go. However, she forced a smile and stood.

"Of course," she said. "I need to get back to the piano anyway."

I nodded, and Rory sat at our table.

Lucy gave us a small curtsy, and then she walked over to the piano.

I waited until she started a song, and then I looked at Rory.

"Talk," I said.

Chapter thirty-three

"It was Tanner Nash that killed Jeremiah," Rory announced. "I was there and saw the whole thing."

I glanced at Ross and looked back at Rory.

"What about Ike?" I asked.

"He wasn't there," Rory replied. "But he was sure mad about it. He even hit Tanner."

"It wasn't Ike's idea?" I frowned.

"No, sir. Tanner acted on his own."

"What happened to Jeremiah's body?" I asked.

"Me, Tanner, and Brock took Jeremiah out and buried him."

"Where?"

"'Bout four miles from headquarters."

I nodded soberly, and it was silent as I thought on things.

"We'll need to see the body," I declared. "Then, we can arrest Tanner for murder and send for Judge Parker."

Ross nodded, and I looked back at Rory.

"Will you testify?"

"Yes, sir," Rory swallowed and nodded.

"It won't be easy," I warned. "When Ike finds out, he might try to kill you so you can't testify."

"You won't protect me?" His eyes grew wide.

"Course we will," I replied. "I just want you to know what you're getting into."

"I've made up my mind," Rory replied stubbornly. "I didn't know what sorta man Ike was when I went to work for him. He's pure evil, Sheriff, and I don't want to work for a man like that."

"I'm glad you feel that way," I said.

Rory nodded emphatically and asked, "So, what's next?"

88

"In the morning, we'll go see Jeremiah's body," I replied.

"What then?" Rory asked.

"Then we'll stash you someplace safe," I replied and stood. "Come on. We're all sleeping at the jail tonight."

Lucy was between songs as we moved to the door, and she glanced curiously at us. Ross waved at her, and we stepped outside.

We went to the house and fetched a few belongings.

Lee and Brian were there, and I explained the situation. Afterwards, Lee smiled and whistled.

"Things are about to get real interesting around here," he declared.

"Looks like it," I agreed, and then we went down to the jail.

There were only two beds in the side room. Ross took one, and I took the other.

"Where do I sleep?" Rory wanted to know.

"You can sleep in one of the cells," I gestured at the back. "Take your pick."

"But I ain't a prisoner," Rory objected.

"You can leave the door open."

Rory frowned and mumbled to himself as he walked to the back.

Chapter thirty-four

We saddled up at daybreak and rode out, with Rory leading the way.

Virgil sat on the porch at the hotel, and I nodded as we passed by.

His face was emotionless, and he didn't acknowledge the nod. Instead, he just stared at me.

Ross noticed the look. He glanced at me, but didn't say anything.

Rory trotted briskly, and we arrived at the unmarked grave midmorning.

The grave still looked fresh. We dismounted, tied our horses to nearby bushes, and unpacked our shovels.

We were silent as we dug. The ground was still loose, and it didn't take us long to uncover the body.

Sure enough, it was Jeremiah.

As I looked down at the remains of my friend, the same feeling that I had felt before came flooding all over me. A violent anger burned deep inside me, and my body trembled with rage.

I must have looked mighty fierce, because Ross and Rory stared at me through wide eyes.

"You all right?" Ross asked.

"Jeremiah was a good man," I said in a hard, cold voice.

"He was," Ross agreed.

"He didn't deserve to die like this," I said, and then I vowed, "Tanner Nash is going to pay for this."

Ross and Rory nodded while I grabbed my shovel.

"Let's cover him back up," I said.

It didn't take us long.

We packed the ground and covered it with stones, and then we packed our shovels and climbed on our horses.

"Ross, you can head back to town," I said. "I'll meet you there later."

Ross nodded while Rory shot me a confused look.

"Are we going somewhere?" He asked.

"I'm going to stash you someplace safe," I replied.

Chapter thirty-five

Rory and I rode toward the Tomlin's headquarters, and we arrived early afternoon.

As we trotted up I spotted Mr. Tomlin and Buster at the corrals, working with some horses.

Rachel and Mrs. Tomlin were on the porch at the main house, and Rachel grinned and waved when she spotted us. I waved back, and Rory waved too.

I frowned at that, but I didn't say anything as we pulled up at the barn.

They stopped working and walked over to us. We dismounted, and I introduced them to Rory.

They shook hands, and already I could tell that Mr. Tomlin was studying Rory with a keen eye.

"What brings you out here this time of day?" Mr. Tomlin looked at me.

I cleared my throat, and then I told them about Jeremiah. I also explained how Rory was my only witness.

While I talked, I noticed that Rory kept glancing at the porch where Rachel was.

Mr. Tomlin was obviously upset about Jeremiah.

"He was a good man and a friend," he declared.

"Yes, sir. He was," I agreed.

"How can I help?"

I nodded at Rory and said, "I was hoping I could leave him here until the trial starts."

"Now hold on," Rory protested. "I don't want to be a burden on anybody."

"You can't stay in town," I replied. "It's too dangerous."

Mr. Tomlin cleared his throat, and we both looked at him.

"Around here, every man pulls his own weight," he declared, and he looked at Rory. "I just lost my two best hands. If you want a job, I could sure use the help. I'll pay you a fair wage in exchange for an honest day's work."

"I'll agree to that," Rory looked eager. "I'm a hard worker, sir, and I'll do the best I can."

"I'm sure you will," Mr. Tomlin said, and added, "Well, get yourself settled. We'll talk more later."

"Yes, sir," Rory said, and Mr. Tomlin and Buster returned to their work.

We went inside the barn, and I showed Rory where to put his horse and gear. After that, I showed him the bunkhouse.

"Now listen," I told Rory sternly. "You're not to leave this ranch for any reason. Understood?"

"I won't."

"I'll come fetch you when it's time to testify," I said.

Rory nodded. He glanced at the porch, and his eyes looked eager as he watched Rachel.

"Is that Mr. Tomlin's daughter?" He gestured.

"Yes," I said shortly.

"She sure is pretty," Rory observed. "Do you know if she's spoken for?"

I frowned disapprovingly and said, "She's spoken for."

"That's too bad," Rory looked disappointed.

"If'n I was you, I would focus on your new job," I said sternly. "You'll find that Mr. Tomlin is a hard man to keep up with."

"I'm looking forward to it," Rory replied, and then he looked at Rachel once more. "That's still too bad," I heard him say softly.

"Well, I'd best be getting back to town," I said abruptly.

Rory nodded, but his eyes never left the porch.

"Remember what I said, 'bout not leaving," I added.

"Sure," Rory said.

I frowned at him, and then I went up to the main house.

***

93

Rachel smiled as I walked up.

"What are you doing here?" She asked.

I explained, and her eyes grew wide.

"I don't like this," she said. "I don't like this at all!"

"Don't worry; I'll be fine," I reassured her.

Rachel looked worried as she studied my face.

"You've changed," she said. "I've never seen you look so stern."

"It's Jeremiah," I said grimly. "Seeing him dead like that-," my voice trailed off.

"I'm sure it was horrible."

"It was," I said, and then I turned towards Desperate. "Well, I'd best be on my way."

"Rondo?" Rachel stopped me.

"Yes?" I looked back at her.

"I know you have a job to do, but don't forget the person you are," she said, and added, "On the inside, I mean."

I smiled faintly and squeezed her arm.

"I'll be fine," I said, and then I stepped into the saddle.

"You be careful," Rachel said wistfully.

"I will," I nodded, and then I rode out.

Chapter thirty-six

It was hot that afternoon, and a thunderstorm began to build as I trotted back to town.

Ross was sitting on the porch at the jail, drinking coffee. I tended to Desperate, and it started raining as I walked across the street and joined him.

We sat there and watched the rain as we drank our coffee.

"Well, looks like we have a job to do," Ross said, and his voice was timid.

"We do," I agreed.

"I don't like our odds, going against a hundred gun-hands."

"More like twenty or thirty," I corrected.

"You say that like it makes a difference," Ross grunted, and added, "No matter how you look at it, there's a lot of them, and only two of us."

"If it comes to it, Lee and Brian will help," I said.

"Four ain't much better."

I took in a deep breath and let it out slowly.

"Arresting Tanner won't be as hard as you think," I said.

"How do you figure that?" Ross looked at me.

It fell silent while I searched for the right words, and Ross looked confused.

"I've got something to say," I finally said. "You might not like it, but you should know."

"What is it?"

"It's about Lucy."

Ross narrowed his eyes.

"What about her?"

I took in another deep breath, and then I explained about her message, Tanner's visits, and also what Lee had said.

His jaw muscles rippled while I talked, and afterwards Ross stared at me with a cold expression.

"I don't believe it," he muttered.

"It's true, Ross," I said. "I'm sorry."

"Lee's a liar."

"Lee's a lot of things," I replied, "but he's not a liar."

"So you believe him?"

I thought on that and nodded.

"I do," I said, and added, "But I ain't judging her past, and I believe anybody can change. But, these visits with Tanner have me concerned."

"There must be a logical reason."

"I hope there is," I said.

"Do you really?"

"Sure I do."

"No, you made up your mind what sorta girl she was as soon as she stepped off the stage," Ross accused. "You've been against her from the start."

"That's foolish talk, Ross."

"Lucy is a good, decent lady," Ross declared. "And, I won't stand for you and Lee to be spreading rumors about her."

I narrowed my eyes at that.

"I'm not spreading rumors," I said. "Only person I've told is you."

"I refuse to believe it."

"You'll believe it tonight," I retorted.

"What do you mean?"

"Tanner usually comes to town right before dark," I explained. "He'll be alone, and we can arrest him."

Ross turned and looked at me, and several seconds passed.

"You're serious," he said.

"We'll meet here just before sunset, and you can see then how serious I am."

Ross snorted and looked down the street. Several seconds passed, and I cleared my throat.

"Ross-," I started to say.

96

"Whatever you have to say, I don't want to hear it," he interrupted.

I scowled at him, but Ross ignored me.

"Fine," I said, and added, "Don't be late tonight."

He nodded abruptly. I stood and stepped out into the street, and the rain fell in sheets.

I hunched my shoulders and kept walking.

Chapter thirty-seven

The rain brought a quick halt to the construction of the hotel. Tools were hastily put under cover, and soaked workers made a dash for the café.

Lee and Brain gestured at me from a corner table as I walked in the café, and I nodded back.

I spotted Virgil sitting alone at a table across the room. He saw me, and our faces were emotionless as we stared at each other.

Several long seconds passed, and neither one of us wavered. Finally, I looked away and joined Lee and Brian.

Lee saw us staring at each other, and he smiled wryly as I sat.

"What?" I looked at him.

"Oh, nothing."

We ate supper, and afterwards Lee pulled out a cigar. He bit off the end, struck a match, and lit it. Meanwhile, Brian and I drank some more coffee.

Occasionally, I glanced at Virgil, and he was just sitting there looking at me while he drank his coffee.

Lee noticed this, and he chuckled.

"What are you waiting for?" He asked as he took a puff on his cigar.

"What do you mean?" I looked at Lee.

"Virgil ain't going away. Sooner or later, you'll have to face him."

"I know that, but I keep hoping there'll be another way," I admitted.

"There ain't," Lee declared. "Not with him. If'n I was you, I'd just kill him and get it over with."

Brian nodded in agreement, and it was silent as I thought on it.

"You might be right," I said softly.

"'Course I am," Lee said, and added, "When the time comes, you watch him. He's good."

"Good as me?" I asked.

"Only one way to find out."

"I know," I frowned, and then I glanced out the window. The rain had stopped, and the sun was going down.

"Well, I'd best be going," I said. "It's going to be a long night."

"Oh?" Lee asked.

I explained, and Lee looked interested.

"Just how mad is Ross?" He asked.

"Mad enough."

"Can you count on him?"

I thought on that and nodded.

"Yes, I think I can."

"Need any help?" Lee asked.

"No, we'll handle it."

Lee nodded and said, "You know where to find us."

"I appreciate that," I said.

I stood and headed toward the door, and I felt Virgil's eyes on me as I walked out.

Chapter thirty-eight

Ross was waiting as I walked up to the jail. I sat beside him, and neither one of us spoke.

Ross took out a plug of tobacco. He bit off a chunk, chewed a bit, and then spat.

We sat in silence for half an hour. Ross finished his chew and glanced at me.

"Well, where is he?" He asked, and there was sarcasm in his voice.

Soon as he said that, I saw movement down the street.

"There he is," I said softly.

Ross turned and looked, and his body stiffened as we watched Tanner ride past us.

Tanner sat up straight in the saddle, and he looked proud and arrogant.

As I watched him, the image of Jeremiah lying dead in the grave returned, and just like that I was hostile and irritable.

"Let's go," I stood.

Ross grabbed his shotgun and followed after me.

Further down the street, I spotted Lee and Brian. They were sitting out on the porch at my house, and they were watching intently.

Tanner was tying his horse to the hitching rail as we walked up. Ross was to my right, and he held his shotgun ready.

"Tanner," I said in a cold, stern voice.

He turned toward us and scowled.

"What do you want?" He demanded.

"You're under arrest for the murder of Jeremiah Batch," I announced. "Drop your gun-belt, or I'll kill you."

"You can't arrest me," Tanner said arrogantly.

"Actually, I can."

My face was blank as I stared at him, and my gun hand hovered over my gun handle. All I needed was an excuse.

Tanner was angry. However, he knew who I was, and he didn't like his odds.

He reached down slowly and unbuckled his gun-belt, and the belt slid to the ground.

"Now walk," I beckoned with my Colt.

Tanner looked sullen as we marched to the jail. We went inside, and I placed him in a cell and shut the door.

"Wait until my father hears about this," Tanner glared at us.

"Be quiet," I told him.

Tanner ignored my remark. He stepped forward, grabbed the cell door, and shook it.

"I want to see my father!" He shouted at us.

Neither Ross nor I replied as we walked back to the front. But Tanner kept yelling, and we could hear him from my office.

I tried to ignore the noise as I looked at Ross.

"You'd best fetch Tanner's gun-belt, and then take his horse to the livery stable," I suggested.

Ross nodded and started for the door, but I stopped him.

"Do you believe me now?"

"About Lucy?" He asked.

I nodded.

"No," he replied, and then he was gone.

I sighed, and then I frowned irritably as Tanner continued yelling.

"Come back here!" He was screaming. "I demand to see my father!"

I walked to the back and stopped in front of his cell, and my face was emotionless as I looked at the man who had killed my friend. The feeling grabbed ahold of me, and I felt a rage down deep.

"What are you staring at?" Tanner sneered at me.

"Be quiet," I warned, and my voice was barely audible.

101

"Who's going to make me!" Tanner fired back.

I smiled at that.

Without a word I unbuckled my gun-belt, hung it on a peg, and grabbed the key to his cell.

"What are you doing?" Tanner's eyes grew wide.

I didn't reply as I opened his cell door and stepped inside.

Tanner grunted and grinned wolfishly.

"You're gonna fight me?" He sneered.

Soon as he said that, I swung my fist and connected with his midsection.

Even though I was small, I was still stronger than most, and my punch hit home hard.

Tanner gasped and doubled over. I followed my punch with an uppercut to his nose, and blood squirted as bones crunched. As his legs buckled, I grabbed his hair and slammed him down.

The air had been knocked out of him, and Tanner groaned as he rolled around on the floor and sucked for air.

"Now be quiet," I said.

Tanner moaned a reply, and I left the cell and locked the door. I returned the key to the peg, grabbed my gun-belt, and buckled it back on. I looked at Tanner once more, and then I went back to the front.

I sat at my desk and enjoyed the silence. A few minutes passed, and Lee and Brian walked in.

"Well, you were right," Lee said. "You didn't need our help."

"Not this time," I said.

"Lucy saw you arrest Tanner," Lee announced. "She was on the balcony."

"How did she take it?" I asked.

"She looked upset."

"I was afraid of that."

"Are you going to tell Ross?" Lee asked.

102

"Nope," I replied. "From here on out, Ross will have to figure things out on his own as far as Lucy is concerned."

"Is he still mad?"

"Yes," I sighed. "He is."

"He'll get over it," Lee grinned.

"I hope so," I said.

***

Lee and Brian didn't stay long. They left, and then Ross showed back up.

I had made some coffee, and Ross poured himself a cup. He took a swig and sat across the room.

It was silent for a bit, and then I cleared my throat.

"We need to talk," I said.

"What about?"

"There's no telling what'll happen next," I said, and added, "I need to know that you and me are good."

"I'm not going anywhere."

It was silent as I studied him, and I nodded slowly.

"All right," I said. "From here on out we sleep at the jail, and during the day one of us needs to be here at all times. If any trouble starts, fire a couple of shots up in the air, and I'll come a-running."

"You reckon Ike will try something?"

"Whether he does or not, we'd best be prepared for it," I replied, and added, "If there is trouble, you stay with Tanner. Any shooting happens, I want you to blow his head off with your shotgun."

"That ain't legal," Ross objected.

"If a prisoner tries to escape, we're supposed to shoot him," I responded.

Ross frowned at that, but didn't reply.

103

Chapter thirty-nine

Ike and Butch sat at the dining room table, eating breakfast, when they heard a commotion outside.

Butch glanced out the window and spotted a rider coming in. He was in a lope, and his horse was lathered with sweat.

Butch met him on the front porch, and after they talked he hurried back inside.

"Well, what is it?" Ike asked as he wiped his mouth with a napkin.

"It's Tanner," Butch explained. "Rondo Landon arrested him."

"What? How come?" Ike scowled.

"For the murder of Jeremiah."

Ike was stunned.

"How did Rondo figure that out?" He asked.

"Somebody must have told him."

Ike grunted. He was irritated, but he managed to stay calm as he thought the situation over.

"What was Tanner doing in town?"

"I'm not sure. He's been riding out almost every night."

"This wouldn't have happened if Rondo was dead," Ike pointed out, and asked, "What's the holdup with Virgil?"

"What I hear, Rondo refuses to face him."

Ike grunted again, and it was silent as he finished his coffee.

"My son is a fool," Ike finally said matter-of-factly. "I'll help, but there are limitations."

Butch nodded but remained silent.

"There was no need to kill Jeremiah," Ike continued. "Without any cows, he would've had to sell eventually. But, as usual, Tanner didn't listen."

Butch nodded again.

"However, he's also the only son I've got," Ike muttered, and he glanced at Butch. "Saddle the horses. We'll ride to town."

"How many men do you want?"

"Nobody else. Just you and me."

Butch frowned at that, but he didn't say anything as he left the room.

Chapter forty

It was a quiet night.

Ross cooked up some breakfast and made coffee the next morning.

He went to the back and gave a plate to Tanner. When he returned, he gave me a questioning look.

"What happened to Tanner? He busted his nose and looks horrible!"

"Did you ask him?" I asked.

"Yes, but he won't say anything."

"He slipped," I explained.

"Slipped?" Ross looked skeptical.

"Sure," I nodded.

Ross frowned at that, but didn't reply.

After breakfast, I left Ross at the jail. I took a stroll around town, and I was just passing the café when two shots bellowed out.

I headed toward the jail in a brisk walk, and as I turned the corner I saw Ross stepping inside.

Ike Nash and Butch Nelson sat a-horseback in the street, facing the jail.

For some reason I glanced up at the balcony of the hotel. Lucy was there, and she was watching with great interest.

I walked up onto the porch, and my gun hand hung free and easy over my gun handle.

"Morning," I said.

"You have my son," Ike said abruptly.

"I do," I nodded.

"Why?"

"He killed Jeremiah Batch."

"Says who?"

"Come to the trial and find out."

While we talked, Lee and Brian walked up. They were armed, and they spread out behind me on the porch.

"You've made a mistake," Ike said.

"That'll be for the judge to decide," I replied.

"I want him released."

"Ain't gonna happen," I shook my head.

"Not even on bail?"

"Nope."

"I've got a lot of men at the ranch," Ike pointed out. "You think you could stop us?"

"Probably not," I admitted, and added, "But if there's any trouble – any at all – then Tanner is going to get accidentally shot. Both barrels."

Ike's face stiffened. He glanced at Butch and looked back at me.

"I'd like to see my son," he said.

"Sure," I nodded.

Ike dismounted, handed Butch his reins, and followed me inside. Meanwhile, Lee and Brian stayed on the porch, and Butch just sat there on his horse in the street.

We walked to the back, and Ike looked displeased when he spotted Ross.

Ross was standing beside Tanner's cell, and his shotgun was pointed at Tanner.

Tanner sat on his bunk, and he looked mad and hopeful at the same time.

"Is that necessary?" Ike beckoned at the shotgun.

"Yes," I replied.

Ike scowled, and then he glanced around, as if he was looking for someone. A disappointed look crossed his face as he turned and looked at Tanner.

"Well, somebody gave you a going over," he observed.

I could tell that Tanner wanted to explain, but he had the sense not to.

Instead, he blurted, "Get me out of here, Pa!"

"Just sit tight, son," Ike said, and then he turned to me. "You want to hold a trial, then go ahead. The truth will come out, and my son will be innocent."

107

"Yes, the truth will come out," I agreed.

Ike didn't reply as he looked back at Tanner.

"I'll see you soon," he said, and he turned and walked back to the front.

"Get me out of here, Pa!" Tanner called out after him.

Ike didn't reply as he walked outside.

Ross and I followed him out, and we stood on the porch and watched as Ike grabbed his reins from Butch.

He didn't say a word as he mounted up, and then he and Butch kicked up their horses.

"What happened inside?" Lee asked as we watched them leave town.

"Not much," I replied, and added, "I think he was hoping for a glimpse of our witness."

Lee nodded, and I glanced up at the balcony of the hotel.

Lucy was still there, and our eyes met. We stared at each other, and her face was hard and cold.

Finally, she turned away and went inside.

Chapter forty-one

Judge Parker lived at Midway. After our altercation with Ike, I sent a man after him.

The rest of the morning passed uneventfully.

Ross eased out at lunchtime and brought us some food from the café, and then he left to go watch Lucy play the piano.

I placed my food on my desk, and then I went to the back and gave Tanner his plate and a cup of water.

Tanner was hungry, and he tore into his meal with a vengeance. I leaned against the bars of the cell and watched him.

"How long until my trial?" Tanner asked.

"Two, three weeks."

"I won't be here that long," he snarled.

"If it makes you feel any better, you just go ahead and think that," I said.

"My Pa will get me out," Tanner declared. "He's an important man."

"I've heard that," I replied. It was silent, and then I asked, "What is your relationship with Lucy Wells?"

Tanner was surprised. He grunted and looked up at me.

"Why do you care?"

"Just curious."

"Me and Lucy is none of your business," Tanner retorted.

I frowned at that.

"All right, have it your way," I said, and I went back up to the front.

I sat at my desk and ate my noon meal, and Ross was back by the time I finished.

"Back so soon?" I asked.

Ross poured himself some coffee and nodded.

"Lucy wasn't there," he said.

109

"Oh? Where was she?"

"I heard she was sick," Ross explained. "So, I went over to the hotel and knocked on her door, but there was no answer."

"Where do you suppose she is?" I asked.

"I don't know," Ross looked worried.

I frowned thoughtfully, but didn't reply.

Chapter forty-two

It was midmorning when Lucy came out of the hotel. She was all dressed up, and she wore her red dress with the low neckline.

She walked down to the livery stable. Mike was there, and she rented a buggy and a team. She also hired Mike to drive it.

"Where do you want to go?" Mike asked her.

"Ike Nash's ranch," she announced.

Mike agreed. He hitched up a team to the buggy and helped her in, and they took off.

Lucy received a lot of attention from the bunkhouse as they arrived at the ranch headquarters. They pulled up in front of the main house, and Mike helped her down.

"Wait for me," she told Mike.

Mike nodded, and Lucy walked up to the front door and knocked. The sound carried loudly, and Lucy heard footsteps.

The door opened, and Butch Nelson looked at her curiously.

"Who are you?"

"I'm here to see Ike Nash," Lucy ignored his question.

"What about?"

"I'll discuss that with Mr. Nash."

Butch grunted. He studied her for a moment more, and then he shrugged.

"Follow me," he said, and he led her to the parlor. "Wait here," he told her.

Lucy nodded, and Butch disappeared down the hallway. He reappeared a few minutes later.

"He'll see you," Butch said, and he showed her to the study.

Ike was sitting behind his desk, and he looked irritable. He frowned as he studied Lucy.

"Who are you, and want do you want?" Ike demanded.

Lucy didn't reply as she sat across the desk. Meanwhile, Butch remained standing at the door, waiting to escort her out.

"I'm here," she announced, "to see what you're doing about my husband."

"And who is your husband?" Ike asked gruffly.

"My husband-," Lucy paused for effect, "-is Tanner Nash, your son. I'm Mrs. Lucy Wells Nash."

Ike was stunned, and he stared at Lucy in disbelief. Butch was just as surprised, and his mouth fell open.

"That is impossible," Ike declared.

"Oh, but it is possible," Lucy replied. "We met last month in Abilene, and we got married before he came back here. I just arrived in town a few days ago."

Ike glanced at Butch, and he frowned in thought.

"I sent Tanner to Abilene on business," Ike recalled.

"That is correct."

Ike sighed and shook his head.

"You are going to be disappointed if you married Tanner for my money," he warned.

"Tanner loves me, and I love him," Lucy replied sharply. "*That* is why we got married."

"I can imagine where he found you," Ike said as he studied her.

"I did not come here to be insulted," Lucy fired back. "Tanner is my husband, and I demand that you do something."

"What exactly do you have in mind?"

"You must have a plan," Lucy objected.

Ike snorted. Meanwhile, Butch looked thoughtful, and he cleared his throat.

"I have a thought," Butch announced. "It's risky, but it might just work."

"Let's hear it," Ike said.

"It'll all depend on you," Butch looked at Lucy.

"I'll do anything," Lucy looked desperate.

Butch nodded, and he carefully laid out his plan. Afterwards, Ike nodded thoughtfully and looked at Lucy.

"Will you do it?"

"Of course," Lucy declared.

"All right then," Ike looked at Butch. "Go talk to Virgil."

Butch nodded, and he and Lucy left the room.

***

Butch saddled his horse, and he trailed along behind the buggy.

They arrived back in town midafternoon.

Mike dropped Lucy off at the hotel, and Butch dismounted and tied his horse to the hitching rail.

They went inside, and Butch asked the hotel clerk for Virgil's room number. They went upstairs and knocked.

Virgil opened the door, and he narrowed his eyes as he studied them.

"What do you want?" He asked in a soft, clear voice.

"Could we come in?" Butch asked pleasantly.

Virgil thought for a moment and nodded.

"Why not."

Vigil stepped back and let them in, and he closed the door behind them.

"I hear you have a problem," Butch said as he glanced around the room.

"What problem?"

"Rondo Landon. He refuses to face you."

Virgil grunted.

"So?"

"We might can help," Butch said.

"How?"

"This is Lucy," Butch introduced. "She's Tanner's wife, but nobody knows that."

113

"I don't care who she's married to," Virgil retorted. "What's that got to do with me?"

"We can help each other get what we want," Butch suggested patiently.

"How?"

Butch explained his plan. Afterwards, Virgil was silent as he thought on it.

"Sounds good in theory," Virgil finally said.

"So you'll do it?" Lucy looked anxious.

"Yes," Virgil agreed, and then he shot Lucy a dark look. "But know this. If anything unpleasant happens, you're on your own."

"I understand," Lucy said.

"I'll go tell Ike," Butch spoke up. "He'll be happy to hear this."

"I don't care what mood Ike is in," Virgil replied. "I just want Rondo."

Butch didn't reply. Instead, he just smiled and nodded as he and Lucy left.

Chapter forty-three

Ross and I stayed at the jail that afternoon. I offered to play a few games of chess, but Ross declined.

I eased out at suppertime and brought back supper. I gave a plate to Tanner, and then we ate at the desk.

Afterwards, I took a stroll around town. All was quiet, so we turned in.

We woke up early, and Ross left after breakfast, saying that he wanted to check in on Lucy.

I frowned at that, but I didn't say anything.

A few minutes passed, and Ross burst back inside. I was drinking coffee, and I spilt some down the front of my shirt as I jumped in surprise.

"You'd better get out here," Ross looked worried.

I frowned as I stood. I checked my Colt and moved to the door.

Virgil Carson was riding down the street, leading two horses. He sat very straight and tall in the saddle, and he looked confident.

One of the horses was Tanner's horse. It was saddled but riderless.

Lucy Wells rode the other horse. Her hands were tied to the saddle, and her feet were tied to her stirrups. Her face was wild with terror, and she looked at Ross with pleading eyes.

Ross swallowed hard and gripped his shotgun.

"Easy now," I said, and Ross nodded.

Virgil held the reins in one hand, and in the other he held his Colt. It was pointed at Lucy's head, and the hammer was pulled back.

Vigil pulled up in front of us, and it was silent while everyone studied the situation. A few seconds passed, and Virgil cleared his throat.

"First thing," he said, "I've got a man with a rifle on the rooftops. Anything unpleasant happen - anything at all - and Lucy is dead."

A look of concern crossed Ross's face while I narrowed my eyes.

"You're bluffing," I said.

"You willing to bet her life on that?" Virgil asked.

"No," Ross spoke anxiously. "We're not."

I shot Ross a dark look, but his eyes were on Lucy.

"I reckon you know what I want," Virgil said. "Turn Tanner loose. Now."

"We give you Tanner, and you give us Lucy," Ross spoke up.

Virgil shook his head no, and it fell silent as I thought on that.

Lucy's eyes were wide with fright as she looked at Ross.

"Help me, please," she whimpered.

Ross nodded and turned to me.

"I'm turning him loose, Rondo," he declared.

"Hold on now-," I started to say.

"No," Ross interrupted, and his face was hard and stern. "We're turning him loose. If that was Rachel, you'd do the same thing."

I frowned, but didn't reply. Meanwhile, Ross moved to the door and disappeared inside.

I looked back at Virgil, and there was an amused look in his eyes.

"I reckon you'll be coming after us," he said.

"You know I will."

"Good," Virgil said, and then Ross and Tanner appeared at the door.

"Get on your horse," Virgil told Tanner.

Tanner snickered as he walked by me.

"I told you I wouldn't be here long," he sneered.

I didn't reply as Tanner mounted up.

"We'll be leaving now," Virgil announced.

"What about Lucy?" Ross demanded to know.

"I'll cut her loose soon as we get out of town."

"You hear that, Lucy?" Ross said. "Everything's going to be all right."

Lucy managed to nod as Virgil backed their horses up.

"I'll see you soon," Virgil looked at me.

"Yes," I agreed, "You will."

Virgil smiled faintly, and they kicked up their horses.

I stood still and watched as they rode out of town. Ross stood beside me, and he looked worried as he watched Lucy.

Soon as they were gone, Ross asked, "Should we search the rooftops?"

"No need," I replied.

"Why not?"

"Because there's nobody there."

Ross frowned in confusion, and I turned and glared at him.

There were a lot of things I wanted to say, but I controlled myself.

"Go find Lee," I said instead.

Ross nodded and took off.

I watched him go, and then I went inside the jail.

Chapter forty-four

Lee, Brian, and Ross arrived at the jail a few minutes later.

"Ross told me what happened," Lee said, and then he complained, "Why does all the good stuff happen when I'm not around?"

Before I could reply, Ross spoke up.

"Virgil said he'd cut Lucy loose, but she hasn't shown up," he said, worried.

"We'll get her back," I replied.

"What are we waiting for?" Ross looked impatient. "Let's be going!"

"There's no need to hurry," I said. "They won't be hard to find."

"How can you be so sure?"

"Because that's what Virgil wants."

Ross didn't understand, and he frowned irritably.

"If Lucy has one bruise on her body-," Ross threatened, and his voice trailed off.

"Why don't you go saddle your horse," I suggested.

Ross didn't reply. Instead, he grumbled something under his breath, and as he left he slammed the door behind him.

Lee grinned and turned to me.

"I told you Lucy was going to bring you trouble," he said.

"I can't believe Ross is being so foolish," I scowled. "He just won't listen to reason."

"Women can affect men that way," Lee said.

"Well, we'd best be going," I said, and added, "Lee, I'd like for you to come along."

"Of course I'm going," Lee replied, and smiled. "You think I'd miss seeing you go up against Virgil?"

I grunted while Lee turned to Brian.

"You'd better stay here and watch over the hotel," he suggested.

Brian didn't like it, but he still agreed.

"You ready?" Lee looked at me.

"One more thing," I replied.

"What's that?"

"You come with us, it's gotta be legal," I said, and I opened the desk drawer and grabbed a deputy's badge.

Brian snickered, and Lee's eyes grew wide.

"Hold on now, Rondo," he protested. "You're gonna ruin my reputation!"

"Good," I said as I tossed the badge to him. "I don't know the words, but you'd better say 'I do' anyhow."

"You're asking too much," Lee objected.

"It'll only be temporary."

Lee frowned and sighed.

"Fine," he muttered. "I do."

I smiled and nodded as I headed towards the door. Meanwhile, Lee grumbled as he pinned the badge on.

"Well, let's be going, Deputy," I said.

Lee scowled as he followed me out the door.

"Word about this gets out," he complained as we headed for the livery stable, "and I won't be able to show my face anywhere."

Chapter forty-five

Just as I suspected, the tracks were easy to follow. They trailed back and forth real slow like, and we made good time.

It was hilly country with long, gentle slopes. There was some brush, but not much.

It was a hot day. We rode for an hour, and sweat streaked down our faces.

I took my hat off and wiped my brow as I squinted at the tracks.

"How far ahead are they?" Ross asked.

"Not far," I said, and I gestured ahead. "They're probably on the other side of that ridge."

"Let's go!" Ross looked anxious.

I glanced at Lee, and then I led out.

There was a steep hill in front of us, and we rode up it. There were several trees at the top, and we dismounted and left our horses amongst the cover. Then, we went over to the edge and looked below.

There was a creek between two hills, and I spotted three horses picketed out. The horses swished their tails as they grazed.

"There they are," I pointed. "By the creek."

Lee had his eyeglass, and he looked through it and nodded.

"I see Virgil," he said.

"What about Lucy?" Ross sounded anxious.

Suddenly, Lee sat up very straight.

"What is it?" Ross asked, concerned.

Lee didn't reply as he lowered the eyeglass.

"Well? Is Lucy all right?"

Again, Lee was silent, and Ross frowned irritably.

Lee looked at me and handed over the eyeglass.

I gave Lee a questioning look, and then I raised the eyeglass and looked through it.

I spotted Virgil. He was by himself, sitting by a campfire drinking coffee.

I swept sideways and spotted Tanner and Lucy.

They were in the middle of the creek. They were in their undergarments, and they were laughing and splashing each other.

"Well?" Ross demanded.

I lowered the eyeglass and looked at Lee, and his eyes twinkled.

Without a word, I handed Ross the eyeglass. Ross looked through it with haste, and it fell silent.

Ross looked for a long time, and the silence was uncomfortable. He finally lowered the eyeglass, and his face was sober.

Nobody knew what to say, but Lee finally cleared his throat.

"Well," he tried to be helpful, "I didn't see any bruises."

Chapter forty-six

Ross looked like he had been kicked in the gut. His face was pale and sober as he thought over the situation.

"The jailbreak was a hoax," he muttered.

"I thought it was," I said.

Ross snorted in disgust and shook his head.

"I feel like a fool."

"I can see how you'd feel that way," I nodded.

Ross muttered something under his breath and looked away.

I looked at Lee, and he couldn't help but grin.

I frowned and shook my head, but Lee's grin grew wider. But then it disappeared as he looked down the hill.

"Virgil's down there, waiting for you," he said.

"That was his plan all along," I said.

"How do you want to handle this?"

"You take Tanner," I said. "I'll take Virgil."

"I want Tanner," Ross suddenly said.

I shot him a startled look.

"You sure?"

"It's my fault he got out," he declared.

I studied Ross and nodded.

"All right, he's all yours," I said, and then I looked at Lee. "I doubt Lucy will be much trouble, but you keep an eye on her."

Lee nodded. I nodded back, and we all checked our weapons.

"Well, let's go," I said, and we moved to our horses and mounted up.

"Everybody ready?" I asked.

Lee and Ross nodded, and we kicked up our horses.

***

122

They spotted us as we rode down the hill.

Tanner and Lucy were walking up from the creek, fully clothed. Lucy uttered a small cry and pointed, and Tanner grabbed his rifle and joined Virgil. Meanwhile, Virgil took a swig of coffee and stood.

We pulled up and dismounted, and we spread out and walked towards them. We stopped when we were about thirty feet away.

Lucy was off to the left, and she glared at us. Tanner stood in front of Ross, and Virgil was in front of me. His gun hand hovered over his Colt, as did mine.

It was silent as we looked at each other, and it was then that the feeling grabbed ahold of me. Just like that I felt calm and ready.

"I told you we would face each other," Virgil said in his soft and quiet voice.

"You've left me no choice," I replied.

"This is for Ben," Virgil declared, and he grabbed for his Colt.

With an easy movement, I palmed my Colt and fired.

Virgil had his Colt out too, and right as he fired my bullet caught him in the chest.

I felt a tug on my shoulder while Virgil went flying backwards.

As Virgil hit the ground he managed to fire again, but the bullet came nowhere close.

With an outraged yell, Tanner swung up his rifle. However, Ross drew his Colt and fired twice before he could get off a shot. Both bullets took Tanner in the midsection, and he flew backwards. He hit the ground and twisted, and he cried out as he died.

I kept my Colt on Virgil. His eyes were starting to glaze over, and blood trickled out his mouth. He made a few gasping sounds, and then he was still.

It was over.

I glanced at Lee, and he looked concerned.

"Hit bad?" He asked.

I examined my shoulder and shook my head.

"No, he barely nicked me."

Lee nodded, relieved. I nodded back, and then I reloaded my Colt and holstered it, as did Ross.

Lucy was just standing there in shock, and Lee covered her with his Colt.

Suddenly, she screamed and ran over to Tanner. Tears ran down her face as she knelt by him. She grasped at him, and then she looked up at us.

"You killed my husband!" She screamed.

We were all startled.

"Husband?" Lee said.

"I'll kill you for this," Lucy vowed, and suddenly her face was twisted and cruel looking. "I'll kill you all!"

"I doubt that," I said, and added, "You're under arrest."

She didn't reply as she looked back down at Tanner.

"Lee, tie her hands," I said.

Lee nodded, and he grabbed some rope from his saddlebags. Meanwhile, I went and got their horses.

While Lee tended to Lucy, Ross helped me with Virgil and Tanner. We threw them over their saddles and tied their hands and feet to the stirrups.

Lee got Lucy on her horse, and he tied her hands to the saddle horn.

"Take Virgil and Lucy back to town," I told Lee as we mounted up. "We'll be along directly."

"Where are you going?" Lee looked curious.

"We're going to take Tanner home."

Lee frowned at that.

"Might be trouble," he warned.

"I doubt it," I replied. "Ike isn't a killer. He hires it done."

Lee looked thoughtful but didn't say anything.

"I'll see you in town," I said.

Lee nodded, and we took out.

Chapter forty-seven

I led Tanner's horse, and Ross rode beside me as we trotted towards Ike Nash's ranch headquarters.

Ross was quiet, and he looked to be deep in thought.

"You all right?" I finally asked.

"I'm upset with myself," Ross admitted. "The way I've been acting has been uncalled for. I'm sorry."

"Apology accepted," I replied, and added, "I should have handled the situation better myself."

"No, it was all me," Ross replied, and then he sighed. "Seems like there's always been some sorta conflict between you and me."

"I know," I agreed, and added, "But I don't want there to be."

"It ain't your fault," Ross replied. "I'm usually the one apologizing."

"Well, I'm sorry things didn't work out with Lucy," I said earnestly.

"I should have listened to you."

"You should have," I agreed, and added, "But you ain't the first man to be fooled by a woman, and I'm sure you won't be the last."

"I just wanted it so bad," Ross said wistfully. "You know what I mean?"

"Yes," I said as I thought of Rachel. "I do."

"It will never happen again," Ross vowed.

"Someday, the right girl will come along," I said reassuringly.

"I'm not sure about that."

"Just listen to me next time," I encouraged.

"Will do," Ross forced a smile.

I smiled back, and it was silent as we trotted along.

"So, how 'bout a game of chess tonight?" Ross asked.

"Sounds good," I smiled.

125

***

We pulled up on the hill that overlooked headquarters.

I could see a few hands loitering around the bunkhouse, and I could also see Ike and Butch, sitting on the porch at the main house.

"Let's go," I said, and we kicked up our horses.

We were spotted as we rode down the hill. I pulled up in front of the main house, and several hands gathered around us. Brock was there, and he glared at me.

Ike and Butch stood, and Ike's face was emotionless as he studied the still form of Tanner.

"Come and get your boy," I told Ike.

Ike didn't reply. He glanced at Butch and nodded.

Butch walked up to me, and I tossed him the reins.

Butch studied me a moment, and then he turned and led Tanner's horse away.

"What happened?" Ike asked in a quiet, stern voice.

"He tried to escape," I replied.

It was silent as Ike thought on that, and then he cleared his throat.

"I thank you for bringing him here," he said.

"Just doing my job," I said.

Suddenly, to my left, I saw Brock facing up to me. His hand hovered over his gun, and it looked like he was about to draw.

I started to make a grab for my Colt, but Ike stopped us.

"Hold it, Brock!" He said sharply.

Brock glared at Ike and scowled.

"You're gonna let him get away with this?"

"I'm a law abiding citizen, Brock," Ike said, and then he looked at me. "I want to make that clear."

Brock scowled. He glared at me once more, and then he turned and walked toward the bunkhouse.

Soon as he was gone, Ike looked at me.

126

"Tanner had friends," he said, "and you can't hold me responsible for anything they might do. I want you to understand that."

"Let's understand one another," I replied abruptly. "I don't like you, and you don't like me. Now, I don't have anything to arrest you on. But, you'll mess up one of these days, and when that happens I'll be coming for you."

Ike frowned and narrowed his eyes.

"We understand one another," he said softly.

"Good," I said.

Ross and I backed our horses away from them, and then we wheeled around and took off in a lope.

Chapter forty-eight

We slowed our pace as soon as we rode over the hill, and Ross looked at me with an amused look.

"You didn't make any friends back there," he commented.

"I have enough friends."

Ross smiled, and asked, "What do you think will happen now?"

I thought on that and shrugged.

"I reckon we'll just have to wait and see."

Ross nodded, and then he changed the subject.

"So, how good was Virgil?"

"He was good," I replied. "Real good."

"Was he better than Kinrich?"

I listened to the question, and I frowned as I thought on it.

"Can't say," I finally said. "Mebbe he was. I'm not sure."

"I believe you're faster now than you ever was."

I smiled, and it fell silent as we trotted on.

"No need to be in a rush, but soon you'll have to move down to the jail," I suddenly announced. "I'll also be talking to Lee and Brian."

"What for?" Ross looked displeased.

I looked at Ross and frowned, and Ross chuckled as he understood.

"You ask her yet?"

"How can I?" I replied. "Since I've been sheriff, I've only seen her a few times. If you've noticed, we've been busy."

"Well, if'n I was you I wouldn't wait too long," Ross said. "She might get tired of waiting and settle on someone else."

Rory came to mind as soon as Ross said that, and I frowned.

"So, are you saying you'd rather live with Rachel than with me, Lee, and Brian?" Ross tried to look hurt.

I didn't think for long.

"That would be correct," I replied, and Ross chuckled.

Chapter forty-nine

Butch and Ike buried Tanner behind the house in their small cemetery.

Butch kept glancing at Ike while they worked. He was solemn and pale, and Butch had never seen him like that.

After Tanner was buried, Ike stood over his grave and looked down.

Butch removed his hat and stood next to him.

"I'm sorry, Ike," he said softly.

"Don't be," Ike said abruptly. "It was a good idea; just didn't work out."

Butch nodded.

"Tanner never would listen to me," Ike declared. "If he had, he'd still be alive."

"What do you want me to do about Lucy?" Butch asked.

"Nothing."

"But she is your daughter-in-law," Butch objected.

"She's not anymore."

Butch nodded and cleared his throat.

"What about Rondo?"

"We'll wait until things settle down," Ike said.

"And then?"

Ike's face glowed with hate as he thought on it.

"I want Rondo to experience the same feeling that I'm feeling now," Ike declared. "We'll find what he loves the most. And then, I'm going to take it from him. He's going to suffer long and hard before I'm through with him."

Butch nodded, but didn't say anything.

"How is Lee's hotel coming along?" Ike changed the subject.

"Should be done soon."

"Good," Ike nodded, and asked, "Figure out Lee's weakness yet?"

"Well, he does like playing cards."

"Hmm," Ike looked intrigued. "That might work."

It was silent as Ike thought on that, and then he nodded.

"Who was that card player we met a while back?" He asked.

Butch thought for a moment.

"Jeremiah Wisdom," he recalled. "He rode with Wade Davis."

"Yes, that's him," Ike nodded. "Send for him. Tell him we have a job."

"Anything else?"

"No, that's all for now," Ike said. He looked at Tanner's grave once more, and then he turned toward the house. "But, I'm just getting started," he declared.

Butch nodded thoughtfully as he followed after Ike.

Chapter fifty

It was late in the day by the time Ross and I got back to town.

We unsaddled our horses, and then we checked on Lucy. Lee had put her in a cell, and she was quiet and sullen.

Ross frowned as he looked at her. He sighed, and then he turned and followed me back up to the front.

"What are we going to do with her?" He asked.

"We've already sent for Judge Parker, so instead of having a trial for Tanner I reckon we'll have one for Lucy," I replied.

Ross nodded.

"What do you suppose will happen?"

"I'm sure she'll go to prison for a long time," I said.

"Good," Ross declared.

"Well, shall we take a stroll around town?" I asked.

Ross nodded, and we went outside.

All was quiet, and afterwards we joined Lee and Brian at the café and ate supper.

We were in good spirits, and we laughed and joked with each other. Afterwards, Lee pulled out a cigar while the rest of us drank more coffee.

"I'm glad to see you with a smile on your face," Lee told me. "I was getting worried."

"Worried? About me?" I looked confused.

"The way you was acting, all moody like, sorta reminded me of Kinrich," Lee explained.

"Seeing Jeremiah like that made me irritable," I admitted. "But, I also promised Rachel that I'd remember who I was. I might have forgotten for a day or two, but I remember now."

"Ross told me about you pistol whipping Brock," Lee said, and added wistfully, "I wish I could have seen that."

132

"Brock won't be forgetting you did that," Brian spoke up.

"I'm sure he won't," I agreed.

"Speaking of forgetting," Lee reached inside his pocket. "I'd better give this back before I forget."

Lee handed me the deputy's badge. I started to put it in my pocket, but then I stopped.

"You sure you don't want to keep it?" I smiled.

"No thanks."

"I might have to call on you again someday," I said.

"I'll be here," Lee said, and Brian nodded.

Epilogue

I cooked breakfast for my three boarders the next morning. Afterwards, I went down to the jail and gave a plate to Lucy.

As soon as Lucy was tended too, I grabbed Rachel's ring from the desk and put it in my pocket. Then, I went to the livery stable and saddled Desperate. I led him outside, mounted up, and rode down the street.

I pulled up in front of Lee and Brian's hotel and studied their progress.

The walls were now up, and they were busy framing the roof. The walls made it look bigger, and I marveled at the size.

Lee looked up and spotted me.

"Going somewhere?" He called out.

"Sure am," I replied, and then I kicked up Desperate.

Lee grinned and waved as he got back to work.

I rode toward the Tomlin's headquarters. Desperate was feeling good and wanting to travel, so we trotted briskly.

I spotted Rachel as I rode up. She was alone on the porch, and she smiled when she saw me.

I took a deep breath and started to ride over. But then Mr. Tomlin spotted me from the barn, and he called out to me.

I frowned hesitantly, but I still turned my horse towards the barn. Rory was also there, and he looked glad to see me.

"What brings you out here?" Mr. Tomlin asked.

"Came to see Rachel," I explained.

A curious look crossed Mr. Tomlin's face, but he didn't say anything.

"I won't be needing you as a witness," I told Rory, and I explained all that had happened.

Afterwards, Rory looked relieved.

"So, it's all over?" He asked.

"For now," I said, and added, "I don't see any reason why Ike would want to bother you, so you can leave now."

Rory looked pleased, but then he frowned as he thought on that.

"Do I have to go?" He looked at Mr. Tomlin. "I like it here."

"'Course not," Mr. Tomlin replied. "The job's still yours if you want it."

"I want it," Rory declared.

"Then it's settled," Mr. Tomlin said, and Rory grinned.

I smiled, and then I glanced at the porch. Rachel was watching us curiously, and my heart skipped a beat.

"If you'll excuse me," I told Mr. Tomlin. "I'd like to go talk to Rachel."

Mr. Tomlin looked at me and smiled.

"Go ahead," he said.

I smiled back and kicked up my horse.

I dismounted in front of the house and tied Desperate to the hitching rail, and Rachel met me at the steps.

My confidence was high, and I walked with determination.

"I overheard some of the conversation," Rachel said, and asked, "What happened with Virgil?"

"I gave him what he wanted," I explained.

Rachel nodded thoughtfully, and then it was silent.

I breathed deeply and looked at Rachel.

"I rode out here to ask you a question," I declared.

"Oh?" Rachel looked startled. "What question?"

Just like that, all my confidence was gone. My stomach tightened, and my heart thumped.

"Well?" Rachel prodded.

"Um," I stammered, and my face turned red.

My throat was suddenly dry, and I coughed and swallowed.

135

There was a twinkle in Rachel's eye. She smiled at me, and just like that all the nervousness was gone.

About the Author

Born in West Texas, Tell Cotten is a seventh generation Texan. He comes from a family with a ranching heritage and is a member of the Sons of the Republic of Texas. He is currently in the cattle business, and he resides in West Texas with his wife, Andi, and their two children.

Tell is the award-winning author of The Landon Saga. His novels have won Gold, Silver, and Bronze in the Readers' Favorite awards, and Tell also won Best New Western in the Laramie Awards and Bronze in the Global ebook awards for CONFESSIONS OF A GUNFIGHTER.

For announcements of new releases and all other information, please like The Landon Saga Page on Facebook https://www.facebook.com/TheLandonSaga Or, you can join The Landon Saga Fan Group https://www.facebook.com/groups/784798154926122/ You can also visit Tell Cotten's website http://tellcotten.wordpress.com/

Acknowledgements
I would like to thank my wife and family for all their help and support. Without them this wouldn't be possible. I'd also like to thank God for the gift of writing.

Special thanks goes out to Mike for the great covers.

And lastly, I'd like to thank Melissa for all her advice, help, and hard work.

Enjoy this excerpt from Tell Cotten's upcoming novel:

Yancy
Book five in The Landon Saga series

In one way or another, I've been a lawman most of my adult life. It's one of the few things in life I'm good at.

I'm also mighty handy with my Colt six-shooter. Not to brag, but I've never been beat. Me being alive is proof of that.

Rondo Landon and Lee Mattingly are still alive too, and I know Lee likes to speculate on who's the best between us.

I reckon it's an interesting question for some, but I've never thought on it much.

My name is Yancy Landon. Like Rondo, I'm smaller than most, and I'm spry and in good shape. Some would call me handsome, although I'm not sure about that.

I've never been one for talking. I think that silence is often the best answer, but most folks never figure that out.

My older brother Cooper is the talker. Tall and wide shouldered, he has an easy-like way about him that I've often envied. Folks admire Cooper because of his character; only reason they admire me is because I'm good with a Colt.

I reckon that's partly the reason why I've never liked being around folks. Strangers always stare at me, hoping to see something, and that gets tiresome.

Us Landons are a well-known family. And, we're also known for our mean temper during times of trouble.

However, it really isn't a temper. Instead, it's just a feeling we all get down deep inside.

It's a feeling of confidence, calmness, loneliness, sharp keenness, and pure meanness all rolled up into one. It also dulls the senses, and many a time we had been hurt and didn't even know it until afterwards.

138

Cooper and I have been riding together for a long time now. I was a lawman back east before the war, and Cooper was my deputy. Then the war broke out, and we joined the Union on the same day.

My name was well-known by the time the war was over. We both received honorable discharges, and we came out west on a cattle drive.

It wasn't long until we were pulled back into service. I was promoted to Captain in the new Texas police force, and we were both assigned to Midway.

Mostly, the Texas police force was corrupt.

The purpose of the police force was supposed to be to fight crime and help with frontier defense, but in most towns that didn't happen. Instead, Governor Davis used his police force to arrest anyone that opposed him.

But I ignored his corrupt ways, and we did our best to treat the folks at Midway fairly. It wasn't easy. We had fought for the North, and there were a lot of folks that disliked us because of that.

J.T. Tussle, a salty old cowman, was one of those that disliked us. He had control of most of the range around Midway, but there were a lot of greedy cattlemen that wanted it. It was a tough fight, and by the time it was over we had finally gained the respect of Tussle and other cowmen.

However, recently that respect had become a bit strained. A while back a stagecoach had been robbed, and a man named Stew Baine killed two men.

Coop and I tried our best, but it was Sergeant Wagons that actually found and killed Stew. He also saved the town from burning while I was gone looking for Cooper.

That made Sergeant Wagons an instant hero. The nickname 'The man who killed Stew Baine' stuck, and the local paper ran several stories about it. There was even talk that a dime novel was being written about it back east.

To make matters worse, Cooper brought back an Indian captive girl named Josie. Judge Parker married them a few days later, and there were some folks that didn't like that. Coop and I were also shot up some, so we couldn't do much.

Soon as we got back on our feet, word came that Richard Coke had defeated Governor Davis.

That was good news. However, that also brought an end to the police force, so that meant that Coop and I were out of a job.

Coop was especially worried about that. He and Josie had some money from selling some pelts, and they were planning on building a cabin. However, they didn't have enough money to finish it. Cooper needed steady pay-days, and he reminded me of that often.

There was now no law in Midway, and I had hoped that the town council would offer me the sheriff's job. Instead, the town council decided to hold an election.

Sergeant Wagons and I both entered the election.

We had two weeks to campaign, but I didn't care for any of that nonsense. Folks already knew who I was, what I stood for, and how I ran things. I figured that was enough.

Sergeant Wagons took a different approach. He knocked on doors and gave speeches whenever possible.

I figured folks would get tired of being bothered, but for some reason they didn't seem to be. It was confusing, because I always got irritated whenever I was around Wagons for very long.

It was now the evening before the election.

The town was all stirred up, wondering who would win. It was a bit too much excitement for me, so I mainly stayed at the jail and drank coffee.

One more day, I thought, *until all this nonsense ends and I'm elected sheriff.*

***

140

That evening I sat out on the porch at the jail. Coop and Josie were off by themselves, busy planning their cabin.

I had just made a fresh pot of coffee. I poured myself a cup, and I put three spoonfuls of sugar in and stirred it with my finger.

I took a swig and sighed in contentment. It tasted sweet, and that's how I liked it.

It was almost dark when Judge Parker walked up.

"Evening, Yancy," he said.

"Judge," I nodded. "When did you get back?"

"Just a while ago," Judge Parker replied, and added, "I figured you might be here, drinking coffee."

"Sit," I offered. "Have some."

Judge Parker poured himself a cup and sat. It was silent as we drank our coffee.

Judge Parker was short and pudgy, with fat fingers. Whatever the situation, he always seemed to look distinguished and important.

We had known each other for a long time. He was a good judge, and we worked well together.

"How'd the trial at Empty-lake go?" I asked.

Judge Parker grunted.

"He escaped before I got there. Rondo and his two deputies took out after him, and one of the deputies killed him."

"Two deputies?" I raised an eyebrow. "I thought Rondo only had one."

"Lee Mattingly was the other deputy," Judge Parker explained. "I believe it was a temporary arrangement."

I scowled as I thought on that.

"Lee Mattingly, a lawman? What's this world coming too?"

"It was a woman that helped Tanner escape," Judge Parker said. "Her, and an older man named Virgil Carson."

"Never heard of him."

"Rondo killed him. As for Lucy, she'll be an old woman by the time she gets out of Huntsville," Judge Parker said. It was silent, and he added bitterly, "That is, if she doesn't escape."

I was confused by that last remark, but I didn't say anything.

"Too bad, Tanner getting killed," Judge Parker continued. "Would have been a big trial. Have you heard of Ike Nash?"

"Some," I nodded.

"Tanner was his son."

"What'd he do?"

"Killed a fella," Judge Parker explained.

I nodded, and it fell silent.

I could tell that Judge Parker had something on his mind, so I waited patiently.

"Ike Nash is more corrupt than Governor Davis was," Judge Parker finally declared.

"Why don't you send him to prison?"

"Can't. He has strong ties all the way back to Washington," Judge Parker said. "I can't touch him until he makes a mistake, and Ike doesn't make mistakes."

"I hear he's been buying up ranches all over Texas," I recalled.

"He's building his own little empire," Judge Parker agreed. "He's also involved in several businesses, all illegal. But, he's got it set up so that nothing can be traced back to him. I've even sent some of his men to prison, but then they escape."

"Huntsville?"

"It's happened twice now."

"Think he has a man inside?"

"Yes," Judge Parker said. "And, that ain't all. He's also been selling guns to the Indians. You remember Wade Davis?"

142

"How can I forget," I said wryly, and I patted my shoulder where he'd shot me.

"He was working with Ike," Judge Parker declared. "I can't prove it, but I know. And now, Ike's got a new partner."

"Why are you telling me all this?" I narrowed my eyes.

Judge Parker took a swig of coffee before he replied.

"I want you to drop out of the sheriff's race," he announced.

I was startled, and I looked at Judge Parker and frowned. "What for?"

"Now that Governor Davis has been defeated, the Texas Rangers are being reorganized," Judge Parker explained. "I'd like for you and Coop to join up. You'd both answer to me."

"Doing what?"

"It's time for this country to unite, Yancy. The war's been over for several years, but men like Ike are still stirring up trouble," Judge Parker said, and declared, "I want to crush Ike. I want to crush his entire operation."

I frowned as I thought on that.

"I needed you before, and I need you again," Judge Parker said. "This is much bigger than the sheriff's job. This is a job that will take months, maybe even years. First, we've got to stop Ike from selling rifles to the Indians. After that, I want you to find out how his men escape from Huntsville. And then, after we've crushed his entire operation, we'll go after Ike himself."

"I'll have to think on it," I replied, and added, "Coop will have to make up his own mind. He and Josie have plans."

"I'm in no hurry," Judge Parker said. "Take all the time you need."

"Whatever we decide, I want to wait until after the election," I said.

"What for?"

"Because I want to win," I admitted. "I can always resign later and pick a replacement."

"Sergeant Wagons can't handle the job?"

"No," I replied. "He can't."

"Nobody else seems to know that," Judge Parker said. "What I hear, a lot of folks like him."

I grunted in response.

Judge Parker chuckled as he stood.

"Well, you and Coop talk it over. Let me know."

"We will," I nodded.

"And remember; this conversation never happened," Judge Parker warned. "Wrong folks in Washington find out about this, then we'll be in prison instead of Ike."

I smiled faintly and nodded.

"You want to win this election, you'd better get out tomorrow and kiss a few babies," Judge Parker suggested.

"I don't like babies."

Judge Parker chuckled, and then he left. Meanwhile, I finished my coffee and went to find Cooper.

Coming soon from Solstice Publishing

For announcements of new releases and all other information, please like The Landon Sage Page on Facebook https://www.facebook.com/TheLandonSaga or you can join The Landon Saga Facebook group https://www.facebook.com/groups/784798154926122/ You can also visit Tell Cotten's website http://tellcotten.wordpress.com/